THE COLOR OF DEATH

"Why are you the color of death?" Chiun asked.

"I know him—that man in the picture," Remo said hollowly. "I killed him. Back in the war. Over twenty years ago. I killed him. He can't be here."

The Master of Sinanju looked at Remo's dazed, pale face. "Enough!" he shouted. "First you see your friend's name scrawled on a dead man's back, now you are claiming that ghosts walk. You cannot be trusted on any mission."

"Try and stop me!" Remo said as Chiun placed himself between him and the door.

Remo was losing his cool . . . he was losing his mind . . . but he wasn't going to lose this battle to go on mission impossible, even if he had to win out over Chiun himself. . . .

THE

#74

Destroyer

WALKING WOUNDED

Created By

WARREN MURPHY & RICHARD SAPIR

A SIGNET BOOK

NEW AMERICAN LIBRARY

For Tom Gray, Cheryl Deep, Lance Deep (USMC), and especially for James P. Kinnon Jr. (US Army Ret.) for taking the time between explosions.

All Soviet military vehicles used in this novel courtesy Veinzat Motion Pictures Rentals, Newhall, CA. Thanks, Andre and Renaud.

PUBLISHER'S NOTE

NAL BOOKS ARE AVAILABLE AT QUANTITY DISCOUNTS WHEN USED TO PROMOTE PRODUCTS OR SERVICES. FOR INFORMATION PLEASE WRITE TO PREMIUM MARKETING DIVISION, NEW AMERICAN LIBRARY, 1633 BROADWAY, NEW YORK, NEW YORK 10019.

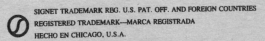

SIGNET TRADEMARK REG. U.S. PAT. OFF. AND FOREIGN COUNTRIES REGISTERED TRADEMARK—MARCA REGISTRADA HECHO EN CHICAGO, U.S.A.

SIGNET, SIGNET CLASSIC, MENTOR, ONYX, PLUME, MERIDIAN and NAL BOOKS are published by NAL PENGUIN INC., 1633 Broadway, New York, New York 10019

First Printing, October, 1988

1 2 3 4 5 6 7 8 9

PRINTED IN THE UNITED STATES OF AMERICA

The footsteps began at the edge of consciousness. Even in sleep, Cung Co Phong recognized them. Somewhere in the deepest recesses of his mind, Phong understood that he slept. He did not want to awaken. Sleep was his only escape. But the familiar, hated footsteps intruded like drumbeats.

Phong awoke in a cold sweat.

The Americans still slept. Nothing seemed to rouse them from slumber anymore. They had been here at Camp Fifty-five so long that they'd ceased to fear the wrath of Captain Dai. But Phong feared Captain Dai. Captain Dai had made the task of breaking Phong's spirit his personal responsibility.

Phong sat up. The hut was still dark. The hammering of his heartbeat was so loud in his ears that it wasn't until the footsteps were nearly to the rattan door that he realized the camp was alive with activity. Men moved about hurriedly. Shovels were at work. And most amazingly, there were trucks. Many of them. And other vehicles. Gasoline had been rationed tightly since long before Phong had been born, up in Quang Tri province.

Whatever had brought the captain in the middle of the night, it was very, very important.

At the sound of the padlock being opened, Phong nudged the others. Boyette, Pond, Colletta, and the others. And finally the big black one, Youngblood, whose snore did not die away until he stopped blinking his bleary eyes at the grass-mat ceiling.

"Huh! What?" Youngblood mumbled. He grabbed Phong's forearm so sharply it hurt. Of all the Americans, only Youngblood had kept his weight. Even in the worst days of captivity, when all there was to eat was fishbone soup, Youngblood never lost a pound.

"Dai," Phong said in his clipped English. "He come."

"Shit! That ain't good news."

The rattan door banged open and a flashlight stabbed at their eyes.

"Up! Up!" said the shadow behind the light. He was tall for a Vietnamese. His sidearm was holstered. He did not fear them enough to draw it.

"What gives?" someone asked in English.

"Up! Up!" Captain Dai barked, stepping in and kicking the nearest man. Phong.

Phong winced. But he said nothing.

They got to their feet, their hands dangling helplessly at their sides. Their gray cotton clothes had no pockets. They never knew what to do with their hands. Single file, they walked out into the night.

The jungle encroached close to the camp, a moving dark wall of primordial foliage. Within the camp, lights blazed. The two-story officers' huts were being dismantled and the sides loaded into the back of flatbed trucks. Tents were coming down. Provisions—sacks of potatoes and rice—were set against a sandbag wall and a human chain of green-fatigued soldiers was relaying them into a canvas-topped truck.

"Looks like we're moving out," Boyette whispered through set lips.

"No talk!" Captain Dai snapped. Although tall for an Asian, he had thin shoulders that might have been cut from a two-by-four. His face was pocked and pitted, the skin so dry it looked dead. His eyes were bright and black—the avid eyes of a crow. A cigarette dangled from his stained, shovellike teeth.

They were quickly surrounded by soldiers, fresh troops

in khaki uniforms, their green pith helmets—adorned only by a red medallion surrounding a single yellow star—sitting low over their merciless eyes.

"Follow!" Dai snapped.

Captain Dai led them around an old T-54 tank, the yellow-starred flag of the Socialist Republic of Vietnam emblazoned on the domed turret.

"Must be big for them to pull a tank from the war zone." Pond had spoken.

"Look again," Youngblood said.

The cannon was false. A wooden barrel painted to look like metal. They walked around it and their hearts stopped.

"Oh, dear God," Colletta moaned.

On the back of a flatbed, they had mounted the steel conex container. Each man knew the conex box intimately. Each of them had spent weeks of solitary confinement in its sterile, stifling interior.

"I ain't going back in there," Colletta suddenly yelled. "No way, man. I ain't! I ain't!"

Youngblood grabbed him and threw him down before the nervous guards could shoot.

"Easy, man. Take it easy. You won't be alone this time. We're all goin' in." He turned to Captain Dai. "Ain't that so? We're all going in."

Captain Dai looked down at them. The soldiers had their AK-47's pointing at them, huddled there on the ground. Youngblood moved his body between their menace and Colletta's flailing, trembling form.

For a long, hot moment even the jungle seemed to hold its breath.

"Up!" said Captain Dai at last.

Youngblood found his feet. "Come on, Colletta," he said. "You can do it."

Colletta sobbed uncontrollably.

"Come on, Colletta. We're going to a better place. You won't be alone, man."

Still crying and trembling, Colletta gathered up his limbs like a clutch of sticks and stood on his feet.

One end of the conex container was opened and they were shoved into its darkened interior. It was warm inside, but not oppressive. Youngblood was the last of the Americans to go in. Phong started to follow, but Captain Dai inserted a boot between his shuffling feet.

Phong fell to his hands and knees. He stayed there because Dai had not given permission to rise.

"You are on your knees now," Dai said in Vietnamese, sneering.

"I tripped," Phong replied in an emotionless voice.

"I need the Americans," Dai said slowly. "I do not need you. Perhaps I will kill you here and leave you for the tigers to eat."

Phong said nothing.

Dai plucked a rifle from the nearest soldier and placed the muzzle against the back of Phong's head. He pressed hard. Phong stiffened his neck. If he was to die here, he would die a man—resisting. His mouth would taste dirt only in death.

"But I will let you live, traitor to the people, if you kneel before me and beg for forgiveness."

Phong shook his head slowly.

Captain Dai sent a round into the chamber.

"You are already kneeling!"

"I tripped."

"Then I will shoot you for your clumsiness," Dai screeched.

Phong said nothing. The pressure of the barrel was more maddening than frightening. He had stared down the barrel of a loaded weapon before and seen Captain Dai's hate-charged face behind it. This way, looking at the red soil of Vietnam and not into the face of death itself, oblivion could be accepted.

Dai pulled the trigger. Phong flinched at the click. But there was no pain, no other sound. Instead, his voice strangled with inarticulate rage, Captain Dai threw the rifle to the ground and picked Phong up bodily.

He flung him into the conex container and the door slammed with a ringing finality.

Inside, the men disentangled themselves and each found a place of his own along the walls. After years of shared captivity, their most basic instinct was to seek a place to call their own.

No one said anything. The truck started up. Other engines joined it. Finally the T-54 tank grumbled and rattled into life. The convoy had started.

No one slept. The novelty of being moved absorbed their attention.

Youngblood's rumbling baritone broke their private thoughts.

"Wherever we're going," he said, "it's gotta be better than where we've been."

"Could be worse," Pond said. "They might be ready to execute us."

"They wouldn't break down the camp to do that, fool," Youngblood scoffed.

"You will not die," Phong said. His voice was distant, stripped of all emotion.

"Yeah?" Youngblood said. He shifted closer to the trembling Vietnamese.

"Dai tell me he need the Americans. I am not needed. You will not die."

"What else did he say?"

"Nothing," Phong said.

"Okay, then. We sit tight. Whatever happens, we just go along. Just like always. We go along and we'll get along."

"You always say that, Youngblood," Pond grumbled. "But what's it ever got us?"

"It's kept us alive," Youngblood said. "I know it ain't much, but it's something."

"I'd rather be dead than kowtow to these stinkin' gooks another day."

"I hear you. But what do you wanna do? We can't cut and run. Charlie owns the whole country now. They're in Cambodia too. There's no place to run to. 'Less you long to go swimming in the South China Sea."

It was a joke but no one laughed.

"They will have to open the door to feed us," said Phong without feeling.

"What're you sayin', man?" Youngblood demanded.

"I am dead man. Dai will kill me if he not break me. He will kill me if he break me. Either way, I am dead man. I have nothing to lose. So I escape."

"Hey, Phong, don't be a stupid gook," Boyette said. "It can't be done."

"No. Mind made up. Listen. Youngblood right. Many men escape, that no good. But one man—not white man—has chance. Leave Vietnam. Go Cambodia. Then Thailand. Is possible for me. Not for American soldier. I go. I tell world."

"That's a laugh," Boyette said bitterly. "If anyone cared, don't you think they would have done something by now? Hell, my kid's gotta be a teenager now. My wife could've remarried three times in the years I've been rotting here. I got nothing to go back to. Face it, we're going to die here."

"No. Show proof. Americans come back. Rescue."

"Sure, Phong. Why don't you just whip out your Kodak and snap our pictures? What? You say you don't have a flashbulb? Aww, that's too bad. Maybe if we ask nice, Captain Dai will shoot more holes in the side of this box to let in a little light."

"Can it, Boyette," Youngblood grunted. "Keep talkin', Phong. How you gonna prove we're here? Tell me. Give us a little hope. I ain't had hope in so long I forget what it tastes like."

In the darkness, Phong reached into the waist of his dirty cotton trousers. He took Youngblood's thick wrist in hand and placed a slim metallic object in his big paw.

"What's this?" Youngblood asked.

"Pen."

"Yeah?"

"I find on ground. Has ink."

"Paper?"

"No. No paper. Have better than paper. Paper get lost."

"Keep talkin', Phong," Youngblood said. "I'm starting to get a whiff of something I like."

The conex stopped at midday. They knew it was daytime because light streamed in through the air holes on one side—air holes that had been made with short bursts from an AK-47.

Someone threw a stone against the side of the conex container and the sound inside rattled their teeth. They all recognized the signal to back away from the door. They crowded to the far end of the dumpsterlike container. All but Phong. The wiry Vietnamese crouched at the door, his body taut, one fist gripping the silver pen like a dagger.

The corrugated door opened outward.

There was only one guard. His rifle was slung across his shoulder. He carried a large wooden bowl of soup—forest greens mixed with red peppers.

Phong sprang on him like a cat.

The guard dropped the bowl, his mouth gulping air. Phong tripped him, kicked at his windpipe, and yanked the rifle from his shoulder. The guard made a feeble grab at the pen—which was suddenly sticking from his sternum like a protruding bone. Then his rifle butt collided with his head. He sat down hard, his head slamming the ground a moment later.

"Atta boy, Phong!"

"Go, man, go!"

"Shut up!" Youngblood snapped. "Phong, close that door. Then get moving! And get rid of the body."

Phong took a last look at his friends, huddling in the rear of the conex, and waved good-bye. Then he swung the conex door closed and dragged the guard's body into the bush.

He stripped the man of his clothes and tied them into a ball. In the guard's pockets were a wallet containing nearly two hundred dong, a military ID card, and a clasp knife. There was a little bag of betel nuts tucked into his right boot. It wasn't much, but it was food. Phong left the boots. They would only slow him down.

The mists were rising off a near hill, and Phong pushed on toward it. He scrambled up the face, using deep-rooted plants for handholds.

At the top, he looked around him. He didn't recognize the terrain and thought perhaps he was in the unfamiliar north. But there was a long ground scar to the west, like those seen often in the old days, when the Americans were in Vietnam. Those early bombing scars had long ago disappeared under new growth.

Phong realized that he was in Cambodia, where the New Vietnamese Army fought Cambodian guerrillas.

Then, down below, the convoy started up. One by one, the trucks wound out of sight, going west, deeper into Cambodia. Even after their sight and sound were an hours-old memory, Phong sat unmoving, waiting for darkness to fall.

When the crickets were in full song, Phong descended. He was very frightened. He was alone in a land where no one could be his friend. The Cambodians would kill him as one of the despised invaders. His fellow Vietnamese would take him for a soldier and force him to fight. And he had no way of knowing how far it was to Thailand. But he was determined.

In the days that followed, Phong lived off tender bamboo shoots and insects. The shoots were plentiful, and he learned to climb into trees above flat rocks and wait for insects to alight. Then he spat red betel-nut juice down to immobilize them. They didn't taste so bad in the juice. But he soon ran out of nuts.

On the fifth day, Phong's resolve to conserve his ammunition for self-defense was shattered. Famished, he killed a small monkey and ate it raw. He carried the bones for three days before he allowed himself the luxury of sucking out the sweet, nourishing marrow.

When he had fired his last bullet, Phong buried the rifle because he was afraid he'd be tempted to chew the wood stock for relief from hunger pains and injure his stomach. By this time, he had changed into the heavier fatigue pants. His cotton prisoners' clothing had been ripped to shreds. He dared not wear the shirt. It would soak up sweat and stick to his back. He took great care at night to sleep on his stomach. He was afraid that the slightest injury to his back would make his journey for nothing.

Phong pushed further west. Time held no meaning for him. He avoided population centers, control points, and the sounds of battle. These detours forced him further and further south.

One night, he smelled salt in the air. It made him dream of fish the next day, when he slept. Hunger was a constant ache in his gut, so he struck out for the south.

Phong came to a river. He hadn't followed it many kilometers before he came across a fishing village whose stilted huts straddled the river. The smells of cooking fish and boiling rice made his stomach heave. But he was too weak to dare steal himself a meal. Instead, he crawled on his stomach to one of the fishing boats on the river and climbed in.

The boat carried him silently down the river. He lay in the bottom of the boat and watched the stars pass overhead. He found a fisherman's net and chewed on it, enjoying the taste of salt. Eventually, he slept.

Phong awoke with the sun. He sat up. The sea around him was indescribably turquoise. Beautiful. And deadly. The South China Sea, some called it. Refugees from the conquered South called it the Sea of Death and Pirates. Many who fled after the fall of the old Saigon government fell victim to its treacherous waters.

Phong hunkered down, unraveling the fish net. Trawlers sat like fat water bugs on the sea's cool surface. If Cambodian, they would ignore him. If Thai, they could be pirates.

Phong cast his net, and when he felt a muscular tugging, reeled it in. He ate the fish greedily, not bothering to kill it. The blood ran down his fingers. It felt wonderful, the cold flesh slipping down his throat. He caught two more, and for the first time in many months, his stomach was full.

Perhaps he would drift down to Malaysia, or the tides might carry him to Thailand, where, if he avoided pirates, he could seek one of the refugee shelters, and then go on to America. He had heard that many refugees spent years trying to leave the camps, but they would take him to America once he showed them his proof. Phong was certain of this.

The screaming changed his mind. It carried across the water as clear as a temple gong. It was a woman, crying out for mercy.

"Khoung! Khoung!"

Others took up her cry. Phong looked up.

A boat wallowed, riding low in the water. Seawater slopped onto its deck. Phong had only to see that to know it was overburdened with cargo. Human cargo. Men, women, and children lined the gunwales. Some had begun jumping into the water.

A fast boat was bearing down on the first craft. It too ran with its decks full. But those decks were filled with men. They brandished pistols, bolt-action rifles, clawhammers, and spiked hardwood clubs. Saffron bands were tied over their brown foreheads.

Thai pirates. The scourge of the South China Sea.

The fast boat came alongside the weaker one, bumped it once with truck-tire fenders, and the two crafts were quickly and expertly lashed together. The pirates descended like raging locusts.

They clubbed, shot, and stabbed the men and the children. The old women were thrown overboard. The younger ones were beaten and pitched over to the pirate ship to be hastily shoved below.

Phong averted his eyes. They were his countrymen, Vietnamese boat people who, even a decade after the war had ended, were risking their lives to escape. And he was helpless.

Phong knew then that he had no hope of floating to Malaysia. He almost jumped overboard, but there was blood in the water now. And blood would bring sharks.

Phong paddled with his hands. He hoped his sense of direction was true.

And the screams continued, growing more distant. "*Khoung! Khoung!*" For hours Phong prayed quietly to his ancestors.

The headland was green and looked cool in the setting sun. The tide brought him closer with agonizing slowness.

Phong would have swum for it, but he remembered what the salt water would do to his back, and so, even though he feared being sighted by coast watchers, he stayed in the boat until at last it bumped shore.

Phong sank the boat with stones and disappeared inland. The ground cooled his bare feet. He had no way of knowing where he was. Thailand, Cambodia—even back in Vietnam.

He'd begun to despair of ever reaching safety. But because it was night, he kept walking, driven less by the will to live than by the memory of his American friends who had been in captivity so long that they had even ceased to hope. Phong was their last hope now. He would not let them down.

He heard the dog bark and he froze. A dog! The bark was distant. Perhaps a kilometer. He listened again, his heart thudding. But the dog did not bark again. Perhaps it had been a hallucination, a trick of the ear.

Phong followed the jungle path. In his mind he sang the old lovers' song of the homeland, "Dark Is the Jungle Path to My True Love's Hut," and he wept with bitter nostalgia for the old Vietnam.

There was a village. And the dog barked again. Once. He had to see if the dog was free, or on a chain. He crawled on elbows and stomach to the village's edge. The dog barked again. It was a happy bark. And then he saw it, yellow and lean and running loose.

A man threw the dog a chunk of meat. Meat! The man was Phong's age, over thirty.

Phong stood up and walked into the village, his hands open and empty. He was safe. There could be no doubt. This was not Cambodia—the Khmer Rouge had virtually eliminated all Cambodian adult men of fighting age. And it was not Vietnam either. No Vietnamese village could afford the luxury of a pet dog. Not with meat in such short supply and dog so tasty.

He was in Thailand.

"I am Vietnamese!" he cried as the villagers circled around him in curiosity. "I am Vietnamese. Take me to refugee camp. I have proof of American MIA. Understand? Proof of MIA!"

2

His name was Remo and he watched as the two men started throwing rocks at each other.

It was a drug deal gone sour. Remo had been sent here to Brownsville, Texas, to take care of Fester Doggins. Fester was a drug smuggler, the man responsible for the shift of cocaine trafficking from Florida to the Texas coast. The DEA had been so successful in their Florida intercepts that the Colombian drug traffickers had to open up a second front in the drug war. Fester Doggins was their American contact. He was moving heavy weight, so Remo had been ordered to terminate his operation and terminate Fester too.

Remo had been waiting at the remote inlet his employer, Dr. Harold W. Smith, had told him Fester regularly used. Remo sat high on an outcropping of rocks, his legs dangling over into space. It gave him a commanding view of the inlet.

Fester had arrived in a chrome-festooned pickup truck with two men. Everyone had guns and wore ostrich-skin cowboy boots and Stetsons pulled low over sun-squint eyes.

The boat came later. It was a yacht, very big and very expensive.

A man in white ducks stepped onto the teak deck of the boat and began speaking to Fester Doggins in Spanish. He was brown-skinned, probably Colombian. Remo didn't understand Spanish, so he waited patiently for the men to conduct their business. His job was to get everyone and make sure the coke shipment never got into circulation. Remo figured that would be easier if they loaded the stuff onto the pickup first. Remo didn't feel like exerting himself today.

But because Remo did not speak Spanish, he had no idea that the rapid-fire exchange between the two businessmen was escalating into an argument. The Colombian snapped his fingers and two men popped up from forward hatches and leveled high-powered rifles at the men on the shore.

Fester's two assistants dived for shelter. One of them made it. The other was chopped down by one of the crewmen.

That was when what Remo considered the rock throwing began.

Bullets flew, ricocheted off rocks, and sprang into the air.

Remo watched unconcernedly. There had been a time in his life when the sound of gunfire made the adrenaline rush through his body. When the sounds of automatic weapons firing meant that random death was in the air. No more. Remo was beyond that irrational fear. He had been trained to think of a firefight as a half-step above a rock fight.

As his trainer in Sinanju had once said:

"A rock is a rock. A big rock thrown by hand is slow. You can see it coming. You can step aside. But a big rock, being big, has a better chance to hit you. Not so a little rock. Like this."

And Chiun, the eighty-year-old Master of Sinanju, held up a small object in one hand and a large stone in the other.

"That's not a rock. That's a bullet," Remo had pointed out.

"It is a rock," Chiun insisted. "It is made of the same material as this other rock. It is smaller. And because it is smaller it has less chance of hitting a target than this large rock."

"Bullets are different, Little Father," Remo had replied. "They travel faster. So they hit harder. They're deadly."

"Are you more dead being killed by a little rock than a big rock?"

Remo had to think about that a minute. "No," he told Chiun. It was long ago. They had been in the gymnasium of Folcroft Sanitarium, where Remo had done his early training. The word "dead" still made him wince in those days. He had been dead in so many ways. Officially dead and dead of mind and body. But through the discipline of Sinanju—the legendary sun source of the martial arts—Chiun had awoken him to his full potential in mind and body. But he was still dead as far as the world knew.

"Good. Now that you understand that dead is dead, I will teach you not to cringe from the little rock just because you imagine it is more fearsome." And Chiun had thrown the large rock at him.

Remo dodged it. Not quite well enough. It struck one elbow right on the funny bone. Remo jumped and howled and clutched his elbow.

And while he was preoccupied with his pain, Chiun picked up a single-shot starter's pistol from a butcher-block table, calmly inserted the bullet, and offered the weapon to Remo, grip first.

"Now you," he said.

Remo took it. "What do I shoot at?"

The old Korean smiled benignly. "Why me, of course."

"I know you. You'll skip out of the way," said Remo, putting the pistol down. "You did that to me the first time we met."

Chiun shrugged. "Fine. Then I will shoot at you." And he picked up the weapon, stepped backward several paces, and drew on Remo.

Remo hit the floor and clamped his hands over his head.

Chiun's smooth brow had wrinkled. "What are you doing? I have not yet pulled the trigger."

"Are you going to?" Remo asked.

"Of course. You surrendered your turn. Now it is mine."

Remo rolled off to one side and curled into a ball so the bullet, if it struck him, wouldn't penetrate to a vital organ.

"You are doing it wrong," Chiun said petulantly. But his hazel eyes held an amused light.

"That is what I was taught in Vietnam."

"You were taught wrong. You do not react until you see the bullet coming at you."

Remo squeezed himself tighter. "By then it will be too late."

"You have seen me dodge these little rocks before."

"Yeah."

"Now you will learn. Stand up."

And because he knew that being shot would be infinitely less painful than disobeying the Master of Sinanju, Remo stood up. His knees felt like water balloons about to break.

"Wait for the bullet," said Chiun, sighting on his stomach.

Remo's hands shot up. "One question first."

Chiun cocked his head to one side like a terrier seeing his first cat.

"Is Smith still going to pay you if I die?"

"Naturally. If you die, the failure will be yours, not mine."

"That's not the answer I was hoping for."

"Hope for nothing," Chiun said. "Expect the worst." And he fired.

Remo hit the floor, the explosive sound of the discharge piercing his ears. He slid along the floor on his stomach, hoping he hadn't been gut-shot.

"Am I hurt?" Remo had asked after a long silence.

"Not unless you are frightened by loud noises."

"How's that?" Remo asked.

"I used a dummy."

Remo's head came up. "Say again."

"Also known as a blank."

Remo climbed to his feet unsteadily. His face was not pleasant.

"You showed me the bullet," Remo said tightly. "That was no blank."

"True," said Chiun, reloading the pistol. "The bullet I showed you is this bullet. It is real. Are you ready?"

"Isn't it my turn again?"

"I have lost track," said Chiun, and fired.

This time Remo's sidewise leap was instinctive. He heard, before the sound of the bullet firing, a cracking noise like a bullwhip lashing out. It was the sound of the bullet passing. Passing! A punching bag behind him exploded in a shower of sawdust.

"I did it!" Remo shouted. "I dodged the bullet."

"I fired wide," Chiun said blandly, reloading the pistol.

Remo's grin squeezed into a lime-rickey pucker. "Not again."

"This time you will look into the barrel of the gun. Look for the bullet."

"I can't. My nerves are shot."

"Nonsense. I have just helped you tune them. You are now truly ready to dodge the harmless little rock."

Remo knew he had no choice. He focused on the black blot of the pistol bore. He tensed. Chiun held his fire. Then Remo remembered his training. An assassin did not tense before danger. He relaxed. He let his muscles loosen, and Chiun nodded with satisfaction.

Then he fired.

Remo saw the muzzle quiver. He saw the black maw turn gray as the bullet filled it. Then he moved. The bullet passed wide and struck a chinning bar with a hollow sound.

Remo grabbed his elbow again, hopping and howling.

"Ouch! Yeoow! What happened? I dodged the bullet. I think."

"True," said Chiun, blowing smoke from the muzzle the way he had seen American cowboys do on TV. "But you did not dodge the ricochet."

"You did that on purpose," Remo growled.

Chiun smiled, wrinkling his wise countenance. "You dance funny."

"On purpose," Remo repeated.

"An enemy would have aimed his ricochet at your heart, not at your funny bone," said Chiun as he replaced the pistol on the table.

Remo looked at his arm. There was no blood. Just a red crease where the bullet had grazed him.

"My turn," said Remo, reaching for the pistol.

"Your turn, yes," agreed Chiun. "But also we are out of bullets."

"Well, at least I proved I can dodge bullets now."

"From a single-shot weapon, yes," said Chiun. "Tomorrow we will try it with a timmy gun."

"Tommy gun. And there's no way I'm going to let you open up on me with a machine gun."

But he had. Not the next day, but three days later, after Chiun had shot at him with a Winchester repeating rifle, a .357 Magnum revolver, and finally a vintage drum-loaded tommy gun. Remo had learned to see the bullets coming, to dodge even the ricochets, until he reached the stage where a man coming at him with a loaded gun no longer tweaked his adrenals but made Remo smile condescendingly. He had learned that a gun was only a clumsy device for throwing rocks. Puny little rocks at that.

And so he watched Fester Doggins and the Colombian throw rocks at one another. Sometimes one of the rocks zipped up toward him. Remo shifted to one side to let the speeding pebble slide past him. He was far beyond the bullet-dodging stage now. His eyes had learned to read the path of a bullet in flight, like a pool hustler calculating where the eight ball would drop. He didn't know how he did it, any more than a runner completely understood the complex relationship between brain impulses and leg-muscle responses that combined to make running happen. He just did it.

When the gunfire died down, there was only the Colombian huddled in the wheelhouse of his yacht and Fester Doggins hunkered down behind his pickup truck. Everyone else was dead. Remo waited. If one killed the other, that would leave only one for Remo to dispose of personally. It would be nice if they polished each other off, but Remo knew that was too much to ask.

While the two men caught their breath and reloaded, Fester Doggins happened to look up. He saw Remo. Remo gave him a friendly little wave.

"Hey!" Fester Doggins called up to him. "Who the Sam Hill are you?"

"Sam Hill," Remo replied. "In the flesh."

"DEA?"

"Nope. Free agent."

"Good. Whose side do you want to be on?"

"Mine," said Remo.

The Colombian, hearing Remo's voice, raised his rifle and drew a bead on Remo's head. Remo knew he was a target when he felt a dull pressure in the middle of his forehead. He looked down at the yacht. He shook his head and waved a finger at the Colombian. "Naughty, naughty!" he admonished.

The Colombian fired once. Remo jerked his head to one side and the bullet shattered the rock face behind him.

Remo picked up a stone not much larger than a quarter and flicked it back at the Colombian. It struck the rifle just ahead of the breech. The rifle broke in two and the Colombian sat down on the deck, hugging his bone-shocked arms and sucking air in through whistling, clenched teeth.

"Where were we?" Remo asked Fester.

"I got a proposition for you," Fester Doggins called up.

"Shoot," Remo said.

"Take care of the Colombian and I'll cut you in on my score."

"How much?"

"One-quarter. We're talking fifty kilos here. It streets at twenty thousand dollars a kilo. What do you say?"

"Who unloads the boat?"

"We do."

"No sale," said Remo. "I don't do heavy lifting. Tell you what—you off-load and it's a deal."

"We're talking a quarter of a million dollars your end. All you gotta do is whack that brown bastard."

"I got a bad back," Remo replied unconcernedly.

The Columbian was struggling with an Uzi submachine gun, trying to make his numb fingers release the safety. Fester noticed this, realized the Colombian had a better shot at him than he had at the Colombian, and yelled his answer.

"Deal! Now, let's go!"

Remo slid off the rock like a spider.

The Colombian stood up suddenly, the Uzi clenched in both hands. He opened up just as Remo's feet touched shore.

Remo wove through the storm of lead as if it were a light rain. Bullets kicked up rock dust, shredded weeds, and hit everything in sight. Except Remo Williams.

Remo stepped lightly onto the boat. The Colombian

stood there, his mouth slack and his gun smoking and empty.

"*Habla español?*" the Colombian asked.

"No. Speak Korean?"

"*No, señor.*"

"Too bad," said Remo, and ignoring the Colombian, he dragged the heavy anchor chain up from the water.

"What are you doing?" Fester Doggins called from behind the pickup. "Stop screwing around. Whack him."

"Hold your horses," Remo said, examining the stubborn anchor. It was one of those that couldn't be raised onto the deck because the chain went through a brass-ringed hole in the bow. The flukes had hung up on the ring. Remo chopped at the fine wood of the gunwale and twisted the brass fittings away. The anchor came loose. It was very heavy and had two flukes. Remo carried it back to the wheelhouse, dragging the chain behind him like the Ghost of Christmas Past.

The Colombian regarded the man approaching him stupidly. He saw a skinny young man with brown hair and deep-set brown eyes carrying an anchor that should have bent him double. And the man carried it in one hand.

Suddenly the skinny man wrapped the flukes around the Colombian's neck and swiftly wound the heavy, slimy chain around the rest of his body.

"*Que pasa?*"

"You," Remo said. "You passa. Good-bye."

And Remo threw the man overboard.

Fester Doggins joined Remo on deck.

"Too bad," Fester said as they watched the bubbles blurp to the surface and eventually stop. "He was my best connection."

"You know what they say," Remo told him. "The thrill can kill." Then he added, "You'd better get started. You have a lot of white stuff to lug."

"No chance," said Fester Doggins, shoving a double-barreled shotgun into Remo's stomach.

"Let me guess," Remo said. "It was you double-crossing the other guy?"

"Yup."

"And now you're double-crossing me."

"Yup," said Fester Doggins. "And at point-blank range there's no way you're gonna skip out of the way of double-0 buckshot."

"Rocks," corrected Remo. "They're just rocks."

"And you're about to eat a bellyful without having to use your mouth," Fester Doggins said as he cocked both barrels.

"One of us is," said Remo, taking the twin barrels in one hand so fast that Fester Doggins could not react. Remo squeezed. The sound was like a tailpipe being run over. Fester looked down.

There was a hitch in both barrels. If he fired now, the blowback would rip his own belly open.

Fester looked at Remo's rail-thin arm, which was bare to the bicep.

"You don't look that strong," he said dully.

"And you don't look that dumb," replied Remo, tossing the useless shotgun into the sea. "Now, load."

Fester Doggins was out of shape. It took him three hours to drag the cocaine onto shore and into the back of the pickup. When he was done, he sat down on the ground and concentrated on his breathing.

Remo got up from his seat in the cabin, where he had been drinking a tall glass of mineral water from the Colombian's well-stocked bar. He jumped onto shore and casually gave the yacht a shove. The yacht slid off and out to sea.

"That was an expensive yacht," huffed Fester Doggins.

"Maybe some deserving orphan will find it," Remo said absently.

"Sure, be casual. You can buy three of them after you resell my coke. Thief."

Remo yanked Fester to his feet and dragged him over to the pickup truck. He set him behind the wheel and placed both hands on the steering wheel, which had a rattlesnake-skin cover. The spokes of the wheel were shiny chrome and there was a series of round holes punched in them. Remo widened two holes with his fingers, inserted Fester Doggins' hands into the holes up to the wrists, and scrunched the holes so that Fester was virtually handcuffed to the steering wheel.

"I don't think I can steer too good with my hands like this," Fester pointed out.

Remo released the hand brake, and the pickup started to roll toward the water.

"Hey, what're you doing?"

"Saying good-bye," said Remo, walking along with the truck. "Good-bye."

"Hey, I'll drown."

"Tough. You sell dope. Dope kills people. Don't you watch the public service messages?"

"Hey, there's a fortune in coke in the back of this thing. It's all yours."

"Don't want it," said Remo, kicking a stone out of the way at the right-front tire. The pickup continued lurching along. Fester Doggins tried to steer away from the water, but the skinny guy kept straightening the wheel.

"Hey, you're throwin' away a fortune."

"So?"

"Can't we deal?"

"No."

"You're gonna let me die?"

"Drown, actually."

The awful truth sank into Fester Doggins' head.

"Well, how about a last toot, then?"

"No time. Here comes the water. Think nice thoughts. They'll be your last."

"Hey, let's talk about this. Tell me what you want! What do I gotta do? Tell me!"

"Just say no."

"Nooo!" said Fester Doggins as the truck's front tires jumped the seawall. The truck slid along its chassis and nosed into the water. It stopped with the rear deck sticking up and the cab entirely underwater. Gasoline mixing with the water made rainbows in the bubbles of Fester's last breaths.

"Too late," said Remo, and sauntered off.

The Master of Sinanju was waiting for Remo at the motel room. Chiun held up a long-nailed finger at Remo's entrance.

Remo walked on cat feet to see what he was watching.

Chiun, reigning Master of Sinanju, had rearranged the furniture since they had checked in this morning. The big double beds were vertically stacked in a corner and the chairs and tables floated in the pool outside the sliding glass doors. Only the big TV remained, and it was set in the middle of the bare floor.

Chiun sat on a *tatami* mat three feet in front of the TV. His wrinkled visage was fixed on the screen. His bright hazel eyes were rapt. He wore a brocaded robe that was heavy enough to be put into service as a throw rug in a British castle.

Remo, seeing that his trainer was intent upon the television, watched curiously.

On the screen, a large black woman in a tent dress smiled into a hand microphone. She was surrounded by a studio audience.

"Isn't that—?" Remo began.

"Hush!" Chiun said.

A colorful graphic appeared over the woman's bovine face as the audience began to applaud vigorously. The graphic read: "The Copra Inisfree Show." Remo was surprised to see Chiun applauding too.

Remo shrugged and sat down next to the Master of Sinanju.

"Today," Copra Inisfree rumbled out in a voice like coffee percolating, "parents who trade their children for rare comic books. After this."

"Yesterday, it was people who worship cheese," Chiun told Remo during the panty-hose commercial.

"Amazing," Remo said.

"Yes, I agree. To think that your government allows this woman to broadcast to the world what imbeciles comprise its citizenry."

"That wasn't what I meant. I saw her in a movie last year. *The Colored People*, or something like that. She was very fat."

"She has been on a diet. She talks about it incessantly."

"That's the amazing part I was getting at. She lost all that weight and she still looks like a lady wrestler."

Then Remo felt Chiun's hand clamp over his mouth. Copra Inisfree was back. She launched into an interview with a young couple who told in heart-rending details about selling their two-year-old girl for a complete set of *The Amazing Spider Man*, only to change their minds when they discovered the fifth issue had a missing page. They spoke tearfully of their protracted legal battle to recover their precious baby. When they were done, the audience sobbed uncontrollably. Copra Inisfree blubbered until her mascara, which looked as if it'd been applied with a lump of coal, streaked her full cheeks.

When the next commercial break came, Remo felt Chiun's hand withdraw suddenly. "I don't think I can take the next segment," Remo said, getting up.

But Chiun did not answer. There were tears running down his cheeks too.

"Oh, brother," Remo said. "I'll see you later."

"Monday it will be interviews with abandoned pets whose masters are missing in Vietnam. Do you think

Smith will let us stay here another few days so that I
may see that program?"

"I doubt it. But I'll ask him."

"Be convincing."

"Why? I don't care about this nonsense."

"You were in Vietnam, were you not? Do you not
care about your missing Army friends?"

"I was a Marine. And Vietnam was a long time ago,"
Remo said coldly as he walked out the door.

3

Copra Inisfree sweltered. The blazing tropical sun seemed only inches from her wide face. It leached precious fluids from deep within her and brought them to the surface as sweat. The sweat dried almost instantly so that vapor drifted off her body in whirling billows. She felt like a steamed ham.

"I don't think I can take any more of this heat, Sam," she complained. "Find me a rickshaw. Hurry."

"This is Thailand, not Hong Kong," said Sam Spelvin, producer of *The Copra Inisfree Show.* "They don't have rickshaws here."

"Then get me a litter or something. Anything. I don't think I can go another step."

Sam Spelvin turned. He stared up the wheeled stairway. Copra Inisfree teetered on the top step. "Copra baby, you haven't even left the plane yet."

"But look at these steps," moaned Copra, clutching the edges of the passenger jet's door for support. "I don't do steps. Don't they have Jetway ramps out here?"

"We're lucky they have an airport. Now, come on, you can do it. Look at me. I'm halfway down with all your luggage."

"What happens if I fall?"

Sam Spelvin wanted to say, "You'll bounce, you ball of blubber," but thought better of it. What he did say was, "I'll catch you, sweets."

"Promise?"

"Absolutely." And as Copra started lumbering down the steps, he prepared to jump out of the way. Just in case her high heels buckled like they did in Paris.

But Copra Inisfree made it to the bottom step without incident. A native taxi was waiting for them.

"Thank goodness," Copra said, collapsing into the back of the open vehicle like a deflating bladder. The car sank on its chassis so far that, once Sam Spelvin squeezed into the front and they got going, the fenders struck sparks off the tarmac.

"Okay," said Sam when they were in traffic. "Here's our itinerary. We're going to the Sakeo relocation camp right away. They're not expecting us until after we check into the hotel. If we hit them early, they won't have time to mount the usual dog-and-pony show. We should get a better guest selection this way."

"Sounds great," Copra said, waving air in her face. "What are we looking for again? I forget."

"The camp is full of Vietnamese refugees who want to come to America. Some of them have been there for years, waiting for sponsors."

"Sponsors! Like the panty-hose people?"

"No, like someone who'll pay their passage to the States, take them in, and help them get started on a new life."

Copra frowned. Even the cleft in her chin frowned.

"Sounds like work," she said. "Why would anyone want to help people they don't even know?"

"Charity."

"Charity is giving money to the poor. Last year I gave twenty thousand dollars to charity," she said proudly.

"You grossed five million smackers last year. You can afford it. Ordinary people can't do that."

"Don't tell me about ordinary people. I deal with them every day, like last week's show on people who believe the same assassin killed Marilyn Monroe and Elvis."

"Some people would argue that the people who guest on your show aren't prime examples of ordinariness."

"If they're not, why are there so many of them?"

"Good point," said Sam. "You know, I was thinking of sponsoring one of these Vietnamese kids myself. They make good domestics."

Copra perked up. "Do they do windows?"

"We can ask," said Sam as the taxi carried them to the wire gates of the relocation camp.

"Look how thin they are," Copra said as she saw the emaciated look of the people watching her from behind the wire. "While we're here, let's ask about diets. Maybe they know some Vietnamese diet secrets."

"They do. It's called starvation."

"I don't think I could handle that. I've got a six-month supply of prime ribs in my basement freezer. If I starved myself, it would all spoil."

"No pain, no gain," said Sam, helping Copra heave herself out of the cab. Actually, he just touched Copra's fat-sheathed elbow and planned to dodge out of the way if she stumbled. The last Copra Inisfree producer had been on a studio elevator when Copra had stepped on—all 334 pounds of her—and the cable snapped. Fortunately for Copra, the elevator fell only one flight to the basement. Unfortunately for the producer, Copra fell on him. Three spinal-fusion operations later, he was getting around with a walker and considering himself lucky.

"You know," Copra mused as they walked through the compound gates, "I'll bet some of these people had to resort to cannibalism to get here. Wouldn't that make a great show? People who ate their relatives to reach America. Let's be sure to ask that question."

"Better hurry," Sam suggested. "Once our government contact finds out we've arrived, it'll be the screened tour."

And like a bull-dozing Zeppelin, Copra Inisfree waded into the crowd. She shook like a Jell-O sculpture in an earthquake.

"You, sir," she bellowed at a middle-aged man. "How did you get out of Vietnam?"

"I walk," the man said.

"And what did you eat to get here?"

"Bugs."

"Good, go stand over there. You, madam. Speak English?"

"A little."

"You're doing fine, honey. What did you eat?"

"Grass. Weeds."

"Okay," Copra shouted. "Listen up, people. Grass-eaters stand off to my left. Bug-eaters to the right. Maybe we can get through this fast."

Hesitantly the Vietnamese milled about until there were two groups, segregated by diet. They smiled in embarrassment.

Copra looked around. There were still some people not on either side. They looked at her in bewilderment.

"You, son," Copra asked a little boy. "What did you eat in Vietnam?"

"Sometimes I eat dog."

"Dog's no good. I don't think our audience would go for that. Besides, we just did a dog-confession show. People who take their dogs to church. Sorry, kid. Next time."

"I don't know, Copra," Sam offered. "I think we can squeeze a show out of dog-eating. We can tape and run it on a delayed basis."

"Good thinking. Hold everything, people," Copra yelled. "Change of plan. Dog-eaters go stand by that tree over there."

Everybody went to stand by the tree, including the grass- and bug-eaters.

"Dog-eating must be popular out here," Copra said with disgust.

"Don't let it throw you, Copra baby. Ask 'em about people."

"Right. Now, can I have your attention again? Did any of you ever eat a person, a fellow human being? It doesn't matter who. It can be a brother or parent or child. Come on, don't be shy. Anyone who ever munched out on the relative? No relatives? How about strangers? Anyone ever eat someone they didn't know?" asked Copra Inisfree, thinking that a show called "Strangers Who Eat Strangers" would fetch an easy thirty share in the ratings.

The crowd regarded Copra Inisfree as if she were voiding in public. Some of the children covered their mouths and giggled.

"No one? Are you sure? Anyone willing to admit to eating a person to get out of Vietnam can come to America with me and be on my show."

Copra was suddenly surrounded by an eager throng. They clutched her arms, plucked at her clothes, and all but pushed her to the ground and made love to her.

"Me! Me! I did! Take me to America now," they squealed.

"Sam," Copra called out from the crowd. "This isn't working." Then she disappeared from sight. The ground shook.

Sam groaned. He yelled for help.

The camp guards scurried up and pulled the refugees off Copra Inisfree. She lay in the dirt like a beached whale. She did not move.

"Copra! Copra! Are you okay?" Sam pleaded.

"Sam, I can't get up."

"Where are you hurt, baby?"

"I'm not hurt, you ninny. I can't get up. Help me."

"Wait right here," Sam told her.

"Don't leave me like this. I just need a strong shoulder to lean on. Just till I find my feet."

"I'll see if there's a crane . . . I mean some strong backs anywhere around here," Sam promised.

While Copra Inisfree lay in the dirt cursing her producer under her breath, a wiry Asian man walked up to her.

"My name Phong," he said.

"Don't bother me unless you had a sex-change operation and want to tell America about it."

"You television lady?"

"Beat it. Unless you can help."

"Wait."

"I have a choice?" Copra asked the sky.

The wiry Asian disappeared. He came back lugging a round, flat stone. He lifted Copra's frizzy head and slipped the stone under her neck.

"I can think of a better pillow," she told him.

"Not done yet," Phong said. He knelt on the ground, his knees resting on either side of her head. For a wild moment Copra thought that this was some exotic kind of Asian sex ritual. She opened her mouth to scream, then remembered that the last time she'd had sex she had to pay for it. She shut her eyes and hoped for the best. Maybe if he did rape her she could go on Donahue and show that piker how to make ratings.

The Asian lifted her head with one hand and Copra felt the cold stone under her neck slide down to the small of her back. Then her head was resting in the man's lap and she started to feel a sense of delicious anticipation. The man took her by the shoulders and pushed with all his strength. His foot jammed the stone into the small of her back and suddenly Copra sensed that she was sitting up.

She opened her eyes.

"Not bad," she said. "I could use a resourceful guy like you."

Phong stood up and took Copra's hand.

"Get ready," he said.

"Whoa. One step at a time. Let me catch my breath. That was a lot of work. Whoosh!"

"Okay," Phong said, squatting beside her. "I have proof."

"Yeah?" said Copra, primping what one fashion magazine called "The Last Afro Haircut Known to Man."

"Proof of MIA."

"Good for you," said Copra.

Sam Spelvin came running up. He had three strapping young men with him. They looked like bodybuilders.

"Copra. I brought help."

"Too late. Thong here is on the job."

"Phong," corrected Phong, jumping to his feet and bowing before Sam. "I have proof of MIA."

"Did you hear that, Copra?"

"Yeah. So what?"

"MIA's. They're one of the hottest issues going. You did two shows on them last year."

"I did? Which ones?"

"You remember. Twins of American POW's, and wives who cheat on their POW husbands."

"POW's? This guy is talking about MIA's."

"Prisoners of war. Missing in action. Same difference. None."

"Why didn't anyone tell me?" Copra complained. "I could have done four shows last year. Brought all the guests back and called the POW's MIA's. Then we wouldn't have had to do that clunker about sex with fish."

"Never mind, Copra baby. Let's hear this guy's story." Sam turned to Phong. "You have proof?"

"Yes, proof of MIA. You wish to see? Take me to America. I show."

"Show us now. Then we'll take you to America."

"Okay," Phong said. And he began to unbutton his shirt.

"Hey, keep your shirt on, pal," Sam Spelvin said. "We're not auditioning Vietnamese bodybuilders here."

"I have proof. I show," Phong said. He finished pulling off his shirt and presented his back to them.

His back was covered with plastic sheeting that was taped on all four sides with silver duct tape. The sheet hung loose and rippled when Phong moved.

"What's this?" Copra asked.

"I put on back when get to camp. To protect. Take away. You see."

Sam shrugged. "Okay, I'll bite," he said, he started to peel away the tape. Phong made painful noises.

"Oh, God, I can't look!" squealed Copra Inisfree. She covered her face with her hands. Her entire head disappeared. "He's probably got some grisly war wound."

"Think again," Sam Spelvin said. He had the sheeting in his hands. He was looking at Phong's bare back. Copra looked too.

Copra was so astonished that she did something that was to become a legend around the water cooler back at her home studio. Without thinking, she got to her feet without anyone helping her. She grabbed Phong, spun him around, and gave him a kiss that almost broke his front teeth.

"Phong baby, you're coming to America."

Phong's dark eyes lit like candles. "I am?"

"I got just one question to ask you."

"What?"

"Do you do windows?"

An hour later Phong found himself seated in the first-class section of a Thai passenger liner. As the Bangkok airport sank beneath the rising wings and they vectored out over the immaculate blue of the Gulf of

Thailand, he made himself a vow that he would not rest until his American friends were one day free to return to their homeland too.

And then all the nervous energy that has sustained him for so long rushed out of him like air leaking from a balloon. Phong lay across three empty seats and went to sleep.

He didn't know what it was that brought him to wakefulness, hours later, in a cold sweat. He thought it had been a nightmare, because he had heard those hated footsteps again.

Phong looked up. The jet was dark, the overhead lights dim. A man's back disappeared into the rest room just ahead of his seat. He hadn't noticed the man before, but because he was awake and his heart pounded in fright, he sat up and waited for him to come out again.

When the man came out, he was rubbing his face as if it were sore. He kept his face averted as he walked past Phong's seat.

But there was no mistaking him. The pock marks on his chin, the way his shoulders stiffened as he walked like the cross-brace of a scarecrow. And the dreadful sound of his footsteps.

Captain Dai. Captain Dai was on this plane.

Phong sank into his seat, trembling. He was not safe yet. Not yet.

4

Captain Dai Chim Sao hated Americans.

An American had killed his father when he was ten years old. He vowed to take his revenge upon all Americans on the day the local political officer brought the news to the family house in Hanoi. He vowed that he would exact a price from all Americans, a hundred times greater than the pain he felt. His mother had long ago run off with another man, leaving him to care for his younger sister. She hadn't cried at first. Not for a week.

But then the American bombers came and the thunder was so great, the ground so shaken by their might, that his sister broke down and wept bitterly and silently for days without end, even long after the bombing stopped.

Nothing was the same after that. When he was twelve, he abandoned his sister just as his mother had abandoned him, and tried to join the People's Liberation Army. But they refused him. So, packing his few possessions, he set off for the south and joined the Vietcong. The Vietcong didn't care that he was a boy. They gave him an old Enfield rifle and two hand grenades and sent him out into the bush.

He shot his first American in the back. The man was in the rear of a patrol. He stopped beside a tree for a drink of canteen water. Dai Chim Sao nailed him to the tree with one shot. The noise brought others. He tossed a hand grenade in their startled faces and jumped into the elephant grass. The grenade made only a small pop. But the screaming carried for kilometers.

They never found him. In the long years of the war, he killed and maimed and ran, never staying to fight because everyone knew there was no way to beat the Americans at war. Ambush and run. Kill and hide. Live to fight again.

When victory finally came, Dai Chim Sao was a man. In the closing days of the war he had enlisted in the North Vietnamese Army, quickly rising to the rank of captain. He swore to kill twice as many Americans as before. But the U.S. troops withdrew back to America and suddenly there were no more Americans to slaughter.

Life seemed purposeless after that. There was the new war in Cambodia, but it wasn't the same. When Captain Dai learned that there was an opening for a political officer at a supersecret outpost, he took it. It was a pleasant shock to discover that he would be in charge of a work camp where despised Americans were being held. He worked them very hard, did Captain Dai.

Seated in the back of the Thai jetliner, Captain Dai wondered if he was about to be given another opportunity to kill Americans. He couldn't kill the American POW's. They were valuable barter. But in America, everyone would be fair game. It would be one gigantic free fire zone.

Dai would have liked to start with the traitor Phong. But in a sealed aircraft, suspicion would immediately fall upon him. He had trailed Phong a long way since he'd been discovered missing from the conex container. Dai was obsessed with Phong, a soft southerner who refused to accept indoctrination, refused to bow or kneel or acknowledge the moral superiority of international socialism.

When Dai had discovered Phong had escaped, he

had beaten the Americans. But they knew nothing. Captain Dai requisitioned a Land Rover and two men and tried to follow Phong's path through the jungle, but a pack of Khmer guerrillas had intercepted them. His soldiers were killed and Captain Dai had been forced to retreat alone.

Reporting to his superior, Vietnam's defense minister, Captain Dai received the first reprimand in a long and glorious career.

"If this Phong reaches a resettlement camp, he will tell the world about the American prisoners," the defense minister had shouted. "We are not prepared for that."

"I will find him," Dai promised stiffly. "Give me time."

"No. We have spies in the resettlement camps. We will alert our people there. If he reaches any of them, we will be notified."

"Permission to eliminate Phong personally."

"Granted. Do not fail."

The call was not long in coming. But when Captain Dai reached the resettlement camp, he was too late. Phong had been taken away by an American journalist.

He shook the spy furiously. "How long ago?"

"Two, three hours ago. They are flying to America."

"Which flight? When?"

"I do not know. But the American journalist is a woman. Big, black, and built like a water buffalo."

Dai had bribed his way onto the Thai plane, and sat in the rearmost row. He was halfway across the Pacific before he realized he had no plan. He had no weapon. Only a forged passport identifying him as a Thai businessman.

Dai had nothing, but he would find a way.

Dai's opportunity came when the plane landed at Los Angeles International Airport.

The big black woman named Copra Inisfree and the hated Phong were the first ones off the plane. The other passengers were made to wait. Dai sneered at the obvious example of American privilege trampling on the rights of others, but the sneer hid worry. What if he lost them in the crowds?

Inside the terminal, Dai realized that that was a silly fear. There was no mistaking the black woman for another. She moved through the terminal surrounded by an entourage of lackeys like a water bug skating across a pond and trailing scum.

Dai followed them to a hangerlike building where hundreds of people milled impatiently around a huge baggage carousel. Dai had no baggage, but he waited anyway.

He spotted Phong squatting on the floor like the peasant he was. Everyone else stood. A few sat on luggage. Phong squatted as if afraid, his eyes shifting nervously.

That would make killing him easier.

Captain Dai slid into the bustling crowds. People, seeing his hard face, instinctively stepped aside. His eyes were mean. No amount of concentration could take that away from him. He drifted closer to his intended victim.

Strangling Phong was out of the question. Too slow. Dai would be stopped. A knife would be best. But he had no knife. There were many blows that killed, but they weren't always certain. Now only three men separated Dai from his intended victim. And still he had no plan.

A ripple of excited chatter went through the throng of people. Dai turned to see what was happening. The first bags were tumbling down the baggage chute. The crowd became a crush. A woman pushed past him and Dai snarled at her indifferent back. Then a smile twisted his pocked face. Her big shoulder bag hung in his face, with a hard metal pen protruding from a slide pocket. It made him think of the body of one of his guards, found dead with a pen such as that plunged into his breastbone.

Yes, a pen would do. Captain Dai eased the pen from the pocket and clicked the point home. A good, strong pen. It would go deep into Phong's soft skin.

Captain Dai shied away from the baggage carousel and sidled up behind Phong, who still squatted away from the others. He had no baggage either. He wouldn't need any where he was going, Dai thought with pleasure.

Captain Dai didn't hesitate. He strode up to Phong from behind and took him by his coarse hair. He snapped his head back and let Phong see his face as his final view of life. Then he brought the pen down toward the man's exposed throat.

In Vietnamese he said, "Now you will die, enemy of the people!"

Phong felt his head snap back. And he saw that face, deeply pocked, eyes black and ablaze. He reached back and grabbed Captain Dai by the back of his knees. Phong squeezed with all his wirelike strength. Captain Dai's knees buckled. He fell awkwardly.

"Help! Help!" Phong cried, grabbing for the pen. He struggled as Dai's hand reached to clamp his mouth shut. Phong took three fingers in his mouth, biting deeply. Dai yelled. The pen slipped from his other hand.

Phong took the pen and raked the man across the eyes. A heavy foot shot up and slammed Phong's jaw shut. He bit his own tongue and felt his mouth fill with blood. He couldn't yell. No one was paying attention to him.

Phong pulled away, sliding along the slick floor like a snake. Captain Dai clutched at his eyes. He stumbled to his feet, lurching blindly for the bank of glass exit doors. He groped for a handle and pushed through, thinking that Phong was not so soft after all.

Phong tried to yell, but his bitten tongue was swelling in his mouth. He couldn't even whisper. He ran for his benefactor, Copra Inisfree, but she was lost in the crowd of airline passengers.

When Phong finally clawed his way to her, he clutched at her oaklike legs.

"Hey, Phong, take it easy," Copra Inisfree boomed. "I know you're grateful to be here in the U.S. of A., but there's no reason to get all worshipful. Though I admire your taste in idols. Hah!"

Phong tugged at the hem of her skirt. He opened his mouth to speak. He was pointing toward the exit doors. Blood poured from his mouth and ran down his chin. The only sounds he made were bubbly gurgles.

Copra Inisfree saw the blood and screamed. Then she fainted. Three people were hospitalized after being pinned under her massive body for nearly an hour. That's how long it took LAX airport officials to summon a forklift to raise her off their moaning bodies.

5

Remo walked the dusty streets of Brownsville until he got tired of walking. He found a phone booth and called his employer, Dr. Harold W. Smith.

He reached Dr. Smith by dialing an evangelical hotline and promising to donate exactly $4,647.88 for the purpose of smuggling Bibles into East Germany.

"Could you repeat that amount, please?" a woman's cool voice asked.

Remo did, and there came a procession of clicks and suddenly he got a ringing line.

"Yes?" said the dry voice of Dr. Harold W. Smith, head of CURE, the super-secret government agency which operated outside of constitutional restrictions.

"Smitty? Mission accomplished."

"That was well-timed," Smith said. "I have something new for you."

"How about a 'Well done' before I grab the next bus?"

"Actually, you'll be flying to New York City. There has been a strange incident at Los Angeles International Airport. I want you to look into it."

"I get it," Remo said brightly. "For security reasons, I'm to fly to New York and do my investigating by phone. That way no one will know it's us."

"No," said Smith. "The people involved are now in New York. Have you ever heard of a television personality known as Copra Inisfree?

"Yeah. She's Chiun's latest passion. I'm not sure 'person' exactly describes her, though. My personal theory is that she's a Macy's Parade balloon and that midgets operate her from inside."

"Highly unlikely," said the humorless voice of Dr. Harold W. Smith.

Remo sighed. He wished he could somehow get a rise out of his employer. "Just give me the broad outlines," he said resignedly.

"Ms. Inisfree has just returned from looking into Asian refugees in Thailand. She has brought back with her a Vietnamese refugee named Phong, whom she claims was attacked upon arrival in this country. Several persons were seriously injured in the attack, so it seems like something more portentous than a publicity stunt. The assailant escaped, and Ms. Inisfree has given a press conference where she promised to reveal dramatic proof of American servicemen still being held prisoner in Southeast Asia on her next show."

"That's an old story," Remo said sourly. "I don't buy it. Vietnam was a long time ago."

"We have nothing on the calendar for you and Chiun. It wouldn't hurt if the two of you were in the studio audience when the supposed evidence is revealed."

"What's the point? Can't you just tape it?"

"You were in Vietnam, Remo. You know those people. Maybe you can tell if this Phong is telling the truth, and while you're at it, evaluate the supposed evidence."

"Waste of time," Remo repeated.

"Your other task will be to protect this man in case he is attacked again."

"I don't do bodyguard work. Ask Chiun. It's beneath Sinanju Masters. We're assassins. Strictly cash-and-carry."

"Your flight leaves in ninety minutes. When you reach New York, call the local dial-a-horoscope and tell the machine you're a Virgo with the sun in Taurus. Further instructions will be given at that time."

Smith hung up.

The first thing Chiun asked when Remo returned to the hotel was the exact question Remo knew he would ask.

"Did you speak with Emperor Smith?"

"Yeah," said Remo. He looked around for something to sit on. Finding nothing, he took up a position near the sliding glass doors.

"Did you ask the permission that I requested?"

"No."

Chiun turned, shocked. "No! A little request such as that? And you forgot. Tell me you forgot. I could forgive you if you forgot. Forgiveness is possible when one is not willfully at fault."

"I made a point of not asking," Remo said, annoyed.

"Then forgiveness is not possible here. I am sorry. Our friendship is over. You may pack your bags and leave now."

"Cut it out, Chiun. I didn't bother asking Smith if you could stay on for *The Copra Inisfree Show*, because he's sending us to see it live."

"Live!" Chiun's facial hair trembled with delight. He brought his long-nailed fingers together in a gentle clap. "We are going to see Copra Inisfree live? In person?"

"It was Smith's idea. I didn't even bring it up."

"No? You do not want credit for this happy gift? You did not suggest it to him?"

"I don't want to go, Chiun."

"Then stay. I will go. You may pack my things as long as you do not have to pack things of your own."

But Remo didn't move a muscle. He was staring out the sliding glass doors. His dark eyes had that inward light of a man who looks into himself and sees something unwelcome.

"What troubles you, my son?"

"This stupid assignment. Smith has his back up because this yo-yo talk-show woman claims she has proof that missing American servicemen are still being held prisoner in Vietnam."

"So?"

"There are no Americans back there. They all got out or were killed in action."

"Why do you say that?"

"'Because I was there, I know. It's a wild-goose chase. It's crap."

"If it is, as you say, crap, why are you angry?"

"It's a stupid idea. There are no Americans alive over there. Can't be."

And Chiun, looking at the dark profile of his pupil, said an odd thing.

"I will pack for both of us."

Remo said nothing. Half an hour later, when the sun set on his impassive face, he hadn't moved from the doors. He might have been staring at his own reflection. If so, his expression said that he did not like what he saw.

6

Their tickets were waiting at the studio door, just as Dr. Smith had promised Remo during his check-in call.

Chiun snatched them out of Remo's hand, examined them critically, and returned one to Remo.

"That one is yours," he said firmly.

"How do you know? They don't have our names on them."

"It has a lower number than my ticket."

An usher led them into the studio, which was nearly full.

"So?" Remo asked.

"It means I will have a better seat."

"Doesn't work that way," Remo said flatly.

The usher stopped at a row near the back and gestured to a pair of vacant seats.

"See?" Remo said, letting Chiun go ahead of him. "We're both in a back row. Smith's idea, I'm sure."

"One sees more from a distance," Chiun said loftily as he pointedly stepped on the toes of several members of the audience who declined to rise as he passed them. He settled into the seat like a bedspread descending over a mattress.

"Right," said Remo. He dropped into the seat beside Chiun. Almost at once, canned music blared an introduction and a scarlet curtain parted to reveal a stage. A camera dollied forward, blocking Remo's view.

"I can't see," Remo complained.

"I can see perfectly," Chiun said smugly.

"I don't care," Remo said as Copra Inisfree stomped onto the stage. "I don't understand what you see in her."

"She's loud, rude, and obnoxious."

"That's what you see in her?"

Chiun shrugged. "Doesn't everybody?"

"I'm not sure," Remo said, looking around the audience. He noticed an unusual number of Asians. Vietnamese. Their faces made shards of old memories dance in his head.

"She reminds me of the Korean jugglers at home," Chiun went on. "Every spring they paint their faces funny colors, throw on rags, and perform tricks for the villagers. Sometimes they pretend to be happy, and other times they weep like faucets."

"Like clowns?"

"Yes. That is the word. I couldn't think of it before. Thank you, Remo."

"I'm starting to get the picture," Remo said.

Up on stage, Copra Inisfree grabbed a microphone and boomed out a greeting. "Today we have a very important show for you, people. I know I promised pets of Vietnam POW's for today, but I have something even better. Our guest is a very brave Vietnamese gentleman who walked barefoot across the war zones of two countries to share his remarkable story with us. Ladies and gentlemen, Mr. Cung Co Phong."

The audience applauded. The Master of Sinanju laughed deliriously. He continued laughing even after the applause died down. Several annoyed faces turned to glower at him. Most of them were Vietnamese.

"Why are you laughing, Little Father?" Remo whispered.

"Because she is so funny. Did you not get the joke about the brave Vietnamese person? A Vietnamese—

brave. Heh, heh. Who ever heard of such a thing? Heh, heh, heh!"

"I think she was serious."

"Nonsense, Remo," Chiun said, composing his kimono skirts. "She is never serious. Her job is to make us laugh. She is Copra the Clown. Listen."

Remo settled in his seat as a short, wiry man stepped onto the stage, shook Copra's hand with a nervous smile, and sat down.

"Before we get into the meat of what you have to tell us, Phong, why don't you repeat for the studio audience what you told me backstage?"

"I come from Vietnam," Phong said slowly.

"We got that part, hon. Skip over to the juicy stuff."

"My English not good. I learn from Americans in work camp."

"Whoa, that's slipping too far ahead. Just tell us about your life in Vietnam."

"I born during war," Phong said carefully. "Both parents work for South Vietnamese government. Both put in camp when I young. I left on own. I try to leave Vietnam. Not have money to pay boat captain. Caught. They say I traitor. Put me in work camp. Later, I am taken to other camp, where Americans are."

"We'll get to that in a minute," Copra said quickly. "Tell us about your escape from Vietnam."

"I stab guard. Run very far, then walk. I walk through Cambodia. Then I take boat. Try to reach Malaysia, but I turn back because of pirates. When I on land again, I find out am in Thailand. Go to relocation camp. Tell story, but no one believe. Everyone say Vietnamese always talk of MIA to get to America. Say I lie. I no lie. I tell truth. I escape to tell world the truth, to get help for my American friends. Americans very good to me in camp. Share rice."

Chiun chuckled. "Did you hear that, Remo? A

Vietnamese telling the truth. Heh, heh. It is against their nature."

"I don't believe him either," Remo said sullenly. "This is a trick. He made up that story just to get on TV. There are no Americans left in Vietnam. None alive, anyway."

"Then why are you not laughing?" asked Chiun.

"Because I don't think it's funny."

"Perhaps you do not appreciate ethnic humor like me."

"I don't appreciate lies. Or people who misuse the memory of dead Americans to get ahead."

Up on the stage, Copra Inisfree jumped up excitedly. Bangles on her wrists tinkled and she toyed with a multicolored scarf that concealed at least two chins.

"Now, before I let Phong tell his story, and it's an exciting one, believe me, I have a story to tell. I found this man in a resettlement camp, and when I heard his story, it was so wonderful, I just couldn't wait to get him on the air. I even agreed to sponsor him in America. And as some of you heard on the news this morning, we were attacked at the Los Angeles airport. We don't know by whom. We're not sure why, but we're pretty sure it was by someone who didn't want Phong to tell his story. Fortunately, no one was killed. Thank God. But several people were wounded and I myself was bruised during the attack."

The audience broke into applause. They cheered Copra's bravery.

"Thank you, thank you," Copra said, waving her bangled hands. "But I am not the hero here. Phong is the hero. Now, Phong," she said, turning to the bewildered Vietnamese, "tell us the truly amazing part of your story."

"In second work camp, I meet Americans. They fought in war. Still there. POW's."

"What were their names, Phong? Do you remember?"

"One man Boyette, another go by Pond. Then there

Colletta, McCain, and Wentworth. And one man, black like you, name of Youngblood."

Remo, who had stopped trying to see over the heads of the studio audience, suddenly sat up in his chair.

"I knew a Youngblood over in Nam. A black guy." His voice was strange.

"Rooty-toot-toot," said Chiun, who was growing impatient. Copra Inisfree had not said anything funny in many minutes.

"How long did you know these men?" Phong was asked.

"Two years. I brought to camp because I know little English. Camp political officer, Captain Dai, he try make me spy on Americans. Tell if they try escape. I not do. Captain Dai get angry. Say he break me, but I stubborn. Not give in. He throw me in hut with Americans. They befriend me and so I become their friend too."

"That all changed a month or so ago, didn't it?" Copra asked.

"Yes. Captain Dai wake us up in night. Camp being moved. We wonder what happening. They put us in conex—long box—take away on truck. Americans think they die, but I know different. I make deal with them. I escape. Promise to come to America, tell world, and get help."

"Now, how do we know you're telling the truth?"

"Have proof," said Phong.

"Now, here it comes, folks. What you're about to see isn't a Vietnamese strip-tease act, but actual, confirmable proof that U.S. soldiers are being held against their will in Vietnam. Show us, Phong."

Phong stood up and gave the audience a polite little bow. He took off his jacket and draped it over a chair. He undid the cuffs of his shirt and removed it.

"Are you ready for this?" Copra said. "Camera, get ready to come in close on this. This is live television, folks. You're about to see history being made. Go for it, Phong baby!"

Phong started to turn around.

"This is degrading," Chiun grumbled. "Have they no shame? Subjecting us to such displays of nudity."

"Quiet, Little Father," Remo said seriously. "I want to see this."

Down near the front, a man leapt up in his seat and pointed at Phong with a shaking finger.

"Die, traitor," he said in Vietnamese, and his other hand swept up. A short burst of gunfire rattled out. Phong, a look of stunned uncomprehension coming over his face, jerked in place as if suddenly touched by a live wire.

More than a dozen tiny holes erupted on his hairless chest. The wall behind him was splashed with red.

For a frozen eternity Phong swayed on his feet; then his legs gave way. He twisted and fell.

The audience gave a sick collective sound when the red monstrosity that was his back came into view.

Then they jumped from their seats and ran for the exits. Excited cries in English and Vietnamese filled the studio. But above them sounded a bellow like a wounded water buffalo. Copra Inisfree's voice.

Remo stood up. "Chiun, the guy with the gun. Stop him. I'll see to Phong."

But the Master of Sinanju was already out of his seat. His sandaled feet hopped to one man's shoulder and then to another's head. His kimono skirts flopping, he floated over the audience, his featherlike leaps alighting only on Vietnamese heads.

Remo, seeing the crowd was panicking, leapt high. He clung to a ceiling cross-brace and, monkeylike, swung into the hanging garden of baby spotlights. Three overhand swings later, he landed on the stage, taking care to keep his back to the TV cameras. His face must not go out over the air.

Remo got down beside the wounded Vietnamese. Phong's body spasmed wildly. Remo knew those were involuntary nerve spasms. The man was not going to make it. His back was cratered with gaping exit wounds. Reno lifted his head and carefully turned him over.

The small holes in Phong's chest dribbled. Sucking chest wounds. Remo had seen them in Vietnam a thousand times. He shook his head no.

"I promise Youngblood," Phong said with effort, clear bubbles breaking over his lips. "Someone go back. Help free Americans."

"I will," Remo said evenly. "I promise."

Suddenly the bubbles breaking at Phong's mouth turned red. His breath wheezed out. His eyes closed.

Remo let Phong's head drop to the hardwood stage and flipped him over onto his stomach. The raw meat that was his back was slick with blood. Near the bottom, over the small of his back, Remo saw the dark lines under the blood.

With his hand, Remo gently wiped the blood away. There were two lines, the name Dick Youngblood, and below that, in Latin, the legend "*Semper Fi.*"

"Dick . . ." Remo said slowly.

On the floor, Copra Inisfree lay spread-eagled. Shaking himself out of his daze, Remo went to her side.

"I'm shot. I've been shot," Copra Inisfree said over and over. "Think of the ratings this must be getting."

"You're fine," Remo said.

"Look at my chest. The blood."

"It's not your blood. It's Phong's. Here, let me help you up."

Copra slapped his hand away. "Don't you touch me with those bloody hands of yours. This dress is a Holstein original. Hand me that microphone."

Frowning, Remo plucked up the mike and put it in her hand.

Copra brought the mike to her lips and, staring at the ceiling, said, "More after this commercial."

Then she dropped the microphone and started to cry.

Remo shook his head in disgust and walked off the stage. The auditorium had been cleared. The cameramen sat calmly behind their cameras as if they were shooting an ant farm and not a human drama. The director picked himself off the floor, saw Copra Inisfree's bloated bulk lying inert, and said in an anguished voice, "Oh, my God, not the star!"

His hands protecting his face from the cameras, Remo slipped out a side exit, looking for Chiun. He found the Master of Sinanju in the lobby. Chiun was standing on a squirming Vietnamese man with a ratlike mustache. The man was shouting imprecations and Chiun quieted him with a tap of one sandaled foot. In his long-nailed hands Chiun held clusters of Vietnamese by their shirt collars.

"Once again," he said bitterly, "you have left me with the dirty job."

Remo lifted his blood-smeared hands wordlessly.

"I suppose there are worse chores than catching lice-infested Vietnamese," Chiun admitted, dropping his handfuls of captives.

"Which one is our guy?" Remo asked.

Chiun shrugged. "How should I know? All Vietnamese have faces like burnt biscuits. Who can tell biscuits apart?"

"I didn't see the killer's face, did you?"

"No. I followed him this far, but they all look alike from the back."

"He wore a blue shirt," said Remo, looking over the men Chiun had captured. Only one of them had a blue shirt.

"You," Remo said. "You're the guy."

"No!" the man protested. "I no shoot. Am American. Naturalized."

Remo reached down and took the man's wrists, one in each hand. He squeezed and the man's fingers went limp. They were empty. Remo bent over and sniffed his palms.

"No gunpowder smell. Let's try the others." Remo checked the rest of them. Their hands didn't give off the telltale smell of burned gunpowder that would have irritated his supersensitive nostrils. Just to be certain, he patted them down. None were armed.

Chiun walked up and down the back of the Vietnamese under his feet.

"This one is not carrying any weapon either," he said.

"You let him get away," Remo said bitterly.

"I tried. Who would have expected so many Vietnamese in one place? Perhaps we should take the head of one of these wretches back to Smith. Who will know the difference?"

"We will," said Remo. "Come on. We have things to do."

"Oh?" asked the Master of Sinanju, stepping off his Vietnamese captive. He wiped his sandals on the plastic foot rug on his way out.

"What things?" asked Chiun curiously, noticing the purposeful set of Remo's face.

"I made a promise back there. And Smith is going to help me keep it."

7

Remo paced his suite at the Park Central Hotel impatiently. He had washed the blood off his hands and changed his clothes. Instead of a white T-shirt and tan slacks, he now wore a black T-shirt and gray chinos.

"Where the hell is Smitty?" Remo asked for the twelfth time. "He said he'd call right back."

"Emperors live by their own sun," Chiun said absently. "It is an old Korean saying." The Master of Sinanju sat on his *tatami* mat, watching Remo with concern. He couldn't remember having seen his pupil so tense. He was acting almost like a typical nerve-frayed American instead of what he truly was, heir to the House of Sinanju, the finest assassins known to recorded history.

"Your breathing is wrong," Chiun pointed out.

"It's *my* breathing."

"You are wasting energy pacing the floor. You should exercise if you desire to work off stress."

"I'm not stressed. I'm impatient. I'm going to call Smitty again," Remo said suddenly, reaching for the phone.

He dialed the correct code on the first try, not even noticing that historical first. He slammed down the phone when he got a recorded message informing him that the number was not in service.

"Damn. He's not even in the office. I got what passes for his frigging busy signal."

Chiun, noticing where the sun sat in the sky, frowned.

"Odd," he said. "The emperor always holds forth at Fortress Folcroft until much later than this. Perhaps he has succumbed to some minor malady."

"Not Smith. He's so bloodless, bacteria die in his mouth."

"Hark!" said Chiun, cocking his head to the door.

"What?" Remo asked peevishly.

"If you would focus on your breathing and not on your strange concerns, you would recognize Emperor Smith's footsteps approaching our door."

"What?" Remo flew to the door. He threw it open.

The shocked, lemony face of Dr. Harold W. Smith stared back at him. Smith wore a white coverall with the name "Fred" stitched into a red oval over his breast pocket. In his right hand he carried a small pressurized tank and nozzle device. His left clutched a shabby leather briefcase.

Smith's high forehead puckered under his thinning white hair. Though the door was open, he knocked loudly.

"What's this?" Remo wanted to know.

"Hotel exterminator," Smith said in a loud and obvious voice. "Open up, please."

"It *is* open," Remo told him.

"Shhh," Smith said. He rattled the doorknob, then said noisily, "Ah, sorry to disturb you, sir. May I come in? This will only take a moment."

Remo rolled his eyes and said, also in a too-loud voice, "Yeah, okay, Mr. Hotel Exterminator. You can come in." But he slammed the door after Smith so hard that Smith dropped his pressurized tank with a muffled thunk.

Smith stripped off the coverall to reveal a three-piece gray suit and mumbled, "Security," as he carried his briefcase over to a round table. He pulled the shades.

"Is this really necessary?" Remo demanded.

"Of course it is, Remo," Chiun inserted, rising in place. "Greetings, Emperor Smith. Your presence here fills us with joy."

"Some of us more than others," Remo said. "I've been losing weight waiting for your return call."

"I've been talking with the President," Smith explained. "Could you please hit the lights?"

Remo switched on the overhead lights. "I prefer sunshine," he added sourly.

"What we're about to discuss is highly classified and must not go beyond this room," Smith said. He retrieved the pressurized tank from the floor, turned a gasket, and toted it to the telephone.

"Oh, come off it," Remo shouted. "You're not actually going to spray for roaches too?"

"This is a debugging unit. It will ensure that our conversation is not eavesdropped upon."

"Fine," Remo said, sinking into the sofa and kicking off his Italian loafers. "While you're at it, sweep my shoes too. The clerk who sold them to me looked shifty."

Smith ignored the remark and finished his circuit of the room. He set down his equipment and joined Remo on the sofa, carefully hitching up his pant legs so the knees wouldn't bag.

"Look at these, Remo," Smith said, pulling a sheaf of glossy photographs from his briefcase. "You too, Master of Sinanju."

Remo looked at the top photo. It showed a misty pattern of green.

"What does that look like to you?" Smith asked.

"An electron-microscope slide of romaine lettuce," Remo said dismissively.

"Yes," Chiun said firmly, "Remo is exactly correct. This is romaine lettuce. I can see the leaf pattern clearly."

"No, these are reconnaissance satellite photos."

"Of romaine lettuce," Chiun added hopefully.

Smith shook his head no.

"No! Remo," Chiun scolded, "you are wrong. And your wrongness influenced my judgment. You will have to forgive him, Emperor, he has been agitated all day. I do not know what the problem is."

"You both know what the problem is," Remo snapped, jumping to his feet. "I told you the problem. I left a friend back in Vietnam. I thought he was dead. Now I know he's still there."

"Only this morning, you were firm in your belief that none of your Army friends remained in Vietnam," reminded Chiun.

"That was before I saw Dick Youngblood's name written on that Vietnamese guy's back. Youngblood was the friend I left behind."

"I have Youngblood's file right here, Remo. Please tell me your story again."

Remo slapped the photograph onto the table.

"Dick Youngblood served with me in I Corps. He and I rotated in together. We served our whole tour together. I guess you could say he was the only true friend I had in those days. We were scheduled to return to the world the same week. I was choppered to a rear area first. I hung around waiting for him to catch up. We were planning to take the same C-130 transport back. Then the VC infiltrated our base camp and we had to dig in. An NVA battalion moved in and started hitting us with rockets. We had to evacuate. I was one of the last ones out. I never saw Dick again. Later they told me that his helicopter was shot down and he was presumed dead. I believed them, so I came home. End of freaking story."

"Did you understand a word he said?" Chiun asked Smith.

"Yes."

"Then could you please translate? I do not understand all the VC's and NVA's and other alphabet nonsense."

"Later," Smith said.

Chiun's mouth puckered. He watched Remo with concern.

"You left the Republic of Vietnam on April 28, 1968," Smith said, glancing at the file. "Is that correct?"

"Sounds right."

"I have the file of a Sergeant Richard Youngblood, reported as missing in action on the twenty-sixth of that month in the province of Ia Drang. A marine. A black. This is his service photo."

Remo took the photo silently. He stared at it a long time.

"That's him. That's sure him," Remo said stonily. "They told me he was dead. Not captured. Dead."

"It's possible they were mistaken," Smith admitted.

Remo threw the photo down and started pacing again.

"Dammit, Smitty. They were wrong! I know they're wrong. That was Dick's signature on the back of that gook."

Chiun started. His papery lips silently formed the word "gook."

"You are quite certain?"

"He was my best friend," Remo shouted. "Don't you understand? My best friend. I know his signature. He was my best friend and I left him behind!"

Suddenly, without any warning, Remo slumped against the window. He tore down the shade and pressed his face and fists to the dying sunlight coming in through the glass. His eyes were squeezed tight. His shoulders shook.

"He was my best friend and I left him to rot in that stinking place." Remo's voice was twisted, hurt.

The Master of Sinanju caught Smith's eye. "He has not been himself since this afternoon," he whispered. "Why is he acting like this?"

"Let me handle this," Smith said quietly.

"Remo," Smith began, walking over to the window.

"The reconnaissance photo I showed you is of a section of the Vietnam-Cambodian border. It shows evidence of a temporary camp on that site. It is one of several such sites our government has been monitoring as possible POW encampments."

"So?" Remo said bitterly.

"This second photo, if you care to look at it, is of the same site. There is no trace of the camp. This photo was taken three weeks ago. After the approximate time the refugee Phong claimed the camp he was incarcerated in had been moved."

Remo opened his eyes and examined the photo.

"It doesn't tell us much, does it?" he said.

"This third one does, however." Smith handed it to Remo. Chiun crowded close, his eyes switching from Remo's face to the photo.

"This site is similar to the first one," Smith continued. "Not exactly, but similar. Notice the ring of huts here. And the latrine trench there. The layout is very similar."

"You think it's the same camp?"

"But moved to a new location, yes. We've determined that no other suspected site has been moved in the same time frame."

Remo looked up at Smith's face. "Then we know where to look."

"Yes. Unfortunately, this new location is on the other side of the border. In Cambodia."

"They're still fighting there."

"It's winding down, but yes, they're still fighting."

"Then we have to get him out of there."

"Patience, Remo. There's more to this story."

"Yes, Remo, there's more to this story," Chiun said gently. "Listen to your emperor."

"I discussed this matter with the President at great length. He informs me that for several months now our government has been in back-channel communication with Hanoi over normalizing relations. There has been movement in the last two months. Considerable movement. The Vietnamese want us to lift economic sanctions as a prerequisite to restoring diplomatic ties. We in turn are demanding a full accounting of all American servicemen known to be missing in action. The Vietnamese officials involved in the negotiations have been dropping hints that they have more than just the remains of our people, but when we press for details, they back off."

"They've got some, all right," Remo said grimly. "I know. That gook's back was covered with names. If he hadn't had so many rounds shot through him, we'd have a list of them. Phong was telling the truth about American POW's. He had them sign their names on his back. That was his proof. I told you that over the phone."

"I expect to receive a full autopsy report and morgue photos later," Smith said. "That will go a long way toward establishing the validity of the signature you saw."

"He wrote 'Semper Fi' at the bottom," Remo said distantly. "That was so like him. Imagine him remembering to do that after all these years."

"My American slang is not good," Chiun told Smith. "I am not familiar with 'Semper Fi.' "

"Short for 'Semper Fidelis,' " Smith said. "Latin for 'Always Faithful.' It's the motto of the Marine Corps."

"Oh," said Chiun, his face puckering. "Army stuff."

"Okay, Smith," Remo snapped suddenly. "You wait for your autopsy report. But while you're waiting, book a flight for Chiun and me. We're going to Vietnam."

"I'm afraid not, Remo," Smith said quietly.

"If you're going to tell me to sit tight while some tight-assed politician negotiates them out, forget it. Dick's been there too damn long as it is. He's not spending any more time in that camp than it will take me to find him."

"We're close to a breakthrough, Remo. The President feels that the POW's may have been moved to Cambodia for some political purpose. The reasoning is that the Vietnamese can't bring them forward without having to admit they've been holding prisoners this long after the war. It's possible they intend to claim our people were found wandering the jungle during the pacification of Cambodia. If we're correct, they could come out any day now."

"I've heard that light-at-the-end-of-the-tunnel speech before. I heard it before I went over there. I heard it after I left. And now you're trying to feed it to me again. Stuff it. This is personal. I'm going in."

"Remo, get a grip on yourself," Chiun said. "You are acting childishly. Vietnam was long ago. It is your past. Your dead past. You cannot go back to it."

"Chiun is right, Remo."

"My gut tells me different," Remo retorted. "I'm going."

"The President and I discussed the possibility of sending you over there. It's out of the question."

"Give me one good reason.

"If we were dealing with a collection of POW's—any POW's—that might be possible, but you've admitted you have a friend among them."

"That's why I'm going."

"No, that is why you must not go."

"Listen to your emperor, Remo," Chiun warned. "He is about to speak wisdom."

"Shut up," Remo snapped. Chiun flinched. To Smith he said, "What does that have to do with anything?"

"You're not thinking clearly, Remo, or it would be obvious to you. When we selected you as CURE's sole enforcement arm, it was because you met certain critical criteria. You were an orphan. You had no close friends. Your background in Vietnam and on the Newark police force indicated a predisposition toward our kind of work. Because our organization officially does not exist, you became our agent who no longer existed."

"No sale, Smitty. You picked me because I was a patriot. Well, Dick is a patriot too. He can keep a secret. I'll just explain the way it is and he'll keep his mouth shut."

"Officially, you are dead, Remo. No one must know different. Suppose you bring your friend back from Vietnam. The publicity would be enormous."

"Dick won't tell. He was so gungee he'd salute Captain Kangaroo."

"Perhaps so, but there are other men with him. You can't trust them. They may not know you, but they will have seen your face, perhaps hear Dick call you by name. No, this is a job for political professionals. Let them handle it."

"I'm going back," Remo said firmly. "You can help. You can not help. Just don't get in my way."

"Emperor Smith will not get in your way," the Master of Sinanju intoned.

"Thanks, Chiun," Remo said sincerely.

"I will get in your way."

Remo spun on the Master of Sinanju. His face was shocked. "Not you too!"

"Look at yourself, Remo," Chiun spat back. "You are not you. You do not talk like yourself. You are nervous, high-strung. All in the space of a few hours. I am watching years of training unravel because you cannot let go of your past. Your dead past."

"Dick Youngblood is my friend. I would never have left him had I known he was alive back there."

"That is guilt talking. But it was not your fault. You were lied to. A soldier should expect that. Listen to Smith. Wait. Your friend will return. You may not see him or speak with him, but you will have the comfort of knowing that he lives."

"I'm going to have the comfort of bringing him back to America," Remo insisted.

Please, Remo. Be reasonable," Smith said. "Here, look at this."

"What is it?" Remo asked, taking a manila folder, but not looking at it.

"A police report on *The Copra Inisfree Show* murder. Ms. Inisfree told the police that Phong confided to her that he knew his airport attacker. Phong claimed it was a Vietnamese political officer named Captain Dai. Ms. Inisfree thinks Dai followed Phong from Thailand to Los Angeles and New York to silence him. That means we have a Vietnamese intelligence agent operating in our country. He was the political officer of Phong's work camp. He could tell us a lot."

"You want me to find him?"

"Alive, he could give us leverage."

"Fine," said Remo. "I'll find him and make him take me to the camp."

"No, find him and hold him. We'll do the rest."

Remo opened the folder. He looked inside. His face went white.

"What is it?" Smith asked.

Chiun snapped the folder from Remo's hand worriedly. He looked at the photo. It was a pock-faced man with ratlike eyes. It showed him standing in the studio audience, pointing a machine pistol. The picture was not clear. It had obviously been copied off a video monitor.

"Why are you the color of death?" Chiun asked.

"I know him. I know that gook," Remo said hollowly. "Oh?"

"Yeah, I killed him. Back in the war. Over twenty years ago. I killed him. He can't be here. He's dead."

The Master of Sinanju looked at the photo again and looked at Remo's dazed, pale face.

"Enough!" he shouted, throwing the folder into the air. Its contents fluttered down around them. "First you see your friend's name scrawled on a dead man's back, now you are claiming that ghosts walk. You cannot be trusted on any mission. You must return to Folcroft immediately. For rest. Then retraining." Chiun wheeled on Smith. "Emperor Smith, others must attend to Remo's assignment. He and I will be occupied, possibly for months."

Smith hesitated. "If you think that's truly necessary."

"Wait a minute—" Remo began.

"You have seen how he acts. You have heard his speech. He speaks like the Remo of old. He is regressing in mind. It is the shock of thinking that his dead friend still lives. Remo has not let go of his past. I must shake it from him."

"I know what I know," Remo insisted.

"You are seeing ghosts from your past—first your friend and now this enemy you admit you killed."

"Try to stop me!" Remo said, lunging for the door.

In a swirl of kimono skirts, the Master of Sinanju left the floor. He sailed across the room, landing in front of the door, barring Remo from leaving.

"Hold!" said Chiun, lifting a warning hand.

"You can't stop me." And Remo came on.

Chiun pulled his hand into a claw and twisted it menacingly. Instinctively Remo's hands swept up to weave in defensive circles.

While Remo's eyes were on Chiun's right hand, his left came out from behind his back and released a wadded ball of paper.

The ball came at Remo's face so fast he couldn't react to it. It struck him on the forehead. Remo's head snapped back as if hit by a sledgehammer and he staggered sideways.

The Master of Sinanju caught him before he kneeled

to the floor, then he carried him to the sofa and gently laid him there.

Doubtfully Smith picked up the ball of paper and unfolded it. He expected to find something heavy inside, like a paperweight. But it was empty. It was the photo of Captain Dai.

"Is he hurt?" Smith asked.

"Of course not. Only stunned. That is why I used mere paper."

"How is it possible to knock a man out with a crumpled sheet of paper?" Smith asked in a wondering voice.

"You throw it very fast," replied the Master of Sinanju as he felt Remo's brow.

8

Remo Williams thought he was back in the bush.

He seemed to be walking point through the elephant grass two klicks south of Khe Sanh—or was it Dau Tieng? Looking around, it was impossible to tell. All elephant grass looked alike—sharp-edged stuff that grew over your head and tangled your feet. Just touching it was like getting a million paper cuts. Behind him the rest of his patrol slogged through the stuff, but only one man trailed close enough to be clearly seen. A black grunt with a gold bead in one nostril. He looked familiar, but Remo couldn't recall his name. His face was a gaunt shell. Only the eyes moved.

Williams pushed forward deliberately, alert for trip-wires. He refused to worry about the pressure-sensitive mines the VC planted everywhere. You don't worry about the things you can't see coming. They are part of the wrong-place-at-the-wrong-time violence of Vietnam, like mortar fire or dysentery. It was no different from being run over back in the world, so you put it out of your mind. But tripwires you could see.

Williams slipped the selector switch on his M-16 from semi to full automatic, counted to twenty, and then went back to semi. It was a ritual he'd practiced since his third month in-country, when he realized that the randomness of sudden death had a mathematical basis. You couldn't know in advance what would pop out of the jungle. It was impossible to predict your chances of surviving a firefight if you walked into it on automatic or semi. But the difference could mean everything. So three times a minute, Williams changed his fire selection. The odds were still virtually even that in a given situation, he'd be in the right mode, but it gave him the illusion of being in control of the uncontrollable. It was just superstition when you got right down to it. But then, everyone was superstitious in Nam.

Williams switched back to automatic fire just as a sound like a sickle swiping through the corn-high grass made the patrol freeze. Williams lifted his hand to signal a halt. Then they heard the percussive chatter of AK-47 rifles.

"VC!" someone shouted.

But it wasn't the Vietcong. They were wearing uniforms. NVA regulars. Williams could see their gray figures moving beyond the chopped grass. And behind them loomed Hill 881 South.

Khe Sanh, Williams thought. *I'm back at Khe Sanh.*

He opened up. Everyone opened up. At first, only the elephant grass fell. Then the black guy with the nose bead went down with both legs cut out from under him. Williams recognized him then. Chappell. Private Lance Chappell, who'd bought it in October '67 when he test-fired an AK-47 he'd found on the trail, unaware that U.S. Special Forces were in the habit of replacing the powder in captured weapons with explosive C4 and leaving them for the Vietcong to find. Chappell was blown to bits.

Lance Chappell. First Battalion, Twenty-sixth Marines, a victim of the Green Berets.

Williams' rifle ran empty. He dropped to one knee, inserted a fresh clip, and flipped the selector back to semiautomatic. The enemy were scattering under the wild return fire. Williams moved forward, firing single shots.

Someone started screaming off in the trees where the North Vietnamese had retreated.

"You greased one, Williams. Good goin'!"

Who said that? I know that voice.

Williams' patrol advanced on the tree line. Return fire was sporadic, ineffectual.

"Anyone see how many there were?" he shouted.

"Three. Three for sure."

"Well, that dink yelling his head off don't count no more," that familiar, ironic drawl said.

They reached the trees, Williams first. He found the wounded NVA soldier lying on his side, no longer screaming, just crying, *"Troi Oi! Troi Oi!"* in a pained voice. Williams' round had caught him in the chest, and pink bubbles broke from his lips with every word. A lung wound.

"Anyone know what he's saying?" he asked.

"Yeah," the ironic voice replied just out of Williams' range of vision. "He's callin' for his God. Probably be meetin' him soon, too."

"Why don't someone speed him on his way?" someone else suggested.

"Good idea." The owner of that familiar voice fired point-blank. The burst went in like a sprinkle of tacks and came out the back like a thresher. The Vietnamese collapsed. The rifleman turned to give Williams a thumps-up sign, and suddenly Williams could make out his grinning face.

Williams smiled back, pleased. It was Ed Repp. The last time he had seen Ed, they were on a two-man patrol on Hill 860. Williams had the point. Ed had called, "Hold up, I'm gonna take a leak," and disappeared into the bush. The explosion came a minute after.

Williams ran in after him. He found Ed's right hand first. It ended in a mass of raw meat flecked with white cartilage. The rest of him lay scattered about a fifty-yard radius. A mine. VC mines released steel pellets that were the equivalent of seventy twelve-gauge shotguns going off under your feet. They did the job.

Williams didn't cry. He didn't react. He just pulled a body bag from his rucksack and started loading. He didn't feel a thing—not even the brief sprinkle that followed the explosion that wasn't the color of rain.

Ed Repp was the last new friend Williams had made in Vietnam. After that, he stopped making friends. They were a bad investment.

Ed Repp, killed while relieving himself near Khe Sanh, Republic of Vietnam, Summer 1967.

But it was a pleasure to see him again. "So, how've you been, Ed?" Williams asked.

Ed stopped smiling and his eyes took on that thousand-yard stare you saw everywhere in the bush.

"Dead. I've been dead," he said quietly.

"Yeah, I know. I was there—remember?"

Ed's eyes came back into focus, and a smile lit up his face, crinkling the corners of his eyes but somehow making him look younger, like a twenty-four-year-old. He was nineteen.

Before he could speak, someone asked, "What about those other two dinks? There might be an NVA base camp nearby." When Williams looked around to see who spoke, the face was vague in the late-afternoon light and he decided it was better not to look closer.

"What do you think, Point Man?" Ed Repp asked lazily. There was a mischievous light in his eyes that Williams recognized.

"Later. We've got a seriously injured man back in the grass. Someone get the bitch box and call in a medevac. Ed, you pop smoke for the dustoff."

The helicopter beat the grass flat as it touched down. They loaded Chappell into the side, and the others climbed aboard too. They waved at Williams as the chopper lifted off. Williams waved back, wondering why he had been left behind.

Then he turned around, and there, inexplicably, were the hills of the Central Highlands off in the distance, green and lush and unspoiled by war, with a heavy mist hanging over them like the breath of angels. Williams just sat down, laid his rifle along his crossed legs, and stared at the beautiful sight until the tears welled in his eyes and he felt a deep, overpowering joy that no one who hadn't lived through Vietnam could understand— and even those who had, had never found the words to describe.

Christ, this place is going to go on forever. Not all the killing, all the politics, screw-ups and bullshit are ever going to change that. Vietnam is eternal and I feel I'm part of it now.

When Remo woke up, he was in an unfamiliar room. The walls were upholstered with some dull padded material. He lay on a large but uncomfortable cot.

Remo sat up on the cot. For some reason, he was having trouble clearing his mind. That hadn't happened to him in a long time. Before CURE, before Sinanju. His whole body felt dull.

A squeaky voice came from the floor.

"Ah, you waken."

"Chiun?"

The Master of Sinanju sat in the corner, on the floor, as always. He had changed into a light yellow robe with high skirts and shortened sleeves. An exercise kimono.

"You remember me? Good," said Chiun, reaching up and tugging on a knotted cord. Outside the heavy, reinforced door, a buzzer blared until Chiun let go of the cord.

"Of course I remember you," Remo said in an annoyed tone. "Why shouldn't I?"

Chiun shrugged. "Anything is possible to one in your state."

"What state is that?"

"New York," said Chiun. "You are in New York.

Heh, heh." But when Remo didn't smile at the Master of Sinanju's little joke, Chiun's parchment face went hard.

"Where am I? Folcroft?"

"Yes. Emperor Smith and I decided you belonged here."

Remo stood up. "In a rubber room?" he asked. The door clicked and Smith stepped in.

"Remo. Master of Sinanju," Smith said by way of greeting. "How are you feeling, Remo?"

"Woozy. What'd you hit me with, Chiun—a brick?"

Chiun produced a ball of crumpled paper from one sleeve, tossed it from right hand to left, and then flicked it to Remo. It sailed up, then sank like a pitcher's curve ball. Remo caught it. He looked at it blankly.

"You're kidding me. It's been years since you were able to tag me with one of your origami beanballs."

"Yes," Chiun said slowly. "That is the sad part."

Smith cleared his throat. "Chiun believes that your training has started to erode, Remo. We brought you here so that he could work with you and sharpen your skills until you are at full potential once more."

"Bulldookey," Remo said. "I'm a full Master now. I'm at my peak. This is just a horseshit scheme to keep me from going off and doing my duty."

"Your duty is to obey your emperor!" Chiun said sharply.

Smith stepped over to Remo and put a hand on his shoulder. "Remo, have you ever heard of delayed-stress syndrome?"

"Flashbacks?"

"Flashbacks are a symptom, yes. In earlier wars, before we understood the psychology of it, the syndrome was known as shell shock. Chiun and I think that today's incident may have triggered a flashback in your mind."

"Before today, I hadn't thought of Vietnam in years. I almost never think about it."

"Some veterans go for years before their first flashback."

"Bull," Remo said briskly. "Vietnam is behind me. I never give it a thought. I don't dream of it. I don't have nightmares about it, I . . ." Remo's eyes went out of focus.

Smith stared at him. "What is it, Remo?"

"Nightmares," Remo said to himself. "Just before I woke up, I was dreaming I was back there. It was real. It was really real. I saw guys I haven't thought about since the sixties."

"See?" Chiun said sternly. "A backflash. You have just admitted to having one."

Remo sat down heavily. He stared at his bare feet. "It seemed so real. I could almost reach out and touch it."

Chiun came to his feet like a parasol opening.

"Do not worry, my son. It will pass. We will train here at Folcroft, like in the old days. We will erase this Vietnam from your mind."

"What about Phong's killer?" Remo asked suddenly. "Did you find him?"

"No," Smith admitted. "We've left the search for the killer to New York authorities. And speaking of this person, we have been able to verify part of Phong's story."

"Yeah?"

Smith drew a grainy photo from a manila folder. "This was FAXed from the Defense Intelligence Agency. It's a photo of a current Vietnamese intelligence officer, Captain Dai Chim Sao. It matches the photo of the man from the Copra Inisfree studio audience."

Remo took the photo.

"It's him," Remo said. "It's really him."

"Come now, Remo," Smith said sharply. "That's a very clear photo. I was certain that once I showed this to you, you would realize your earlier identification was in error. Are you still insisting that this is the man you killed during the war?"

"We didn't know his name," Remo said. "We called him Captain Spook, because we suspected he was NVA intelligence. He was a legend. Sometimes he was dressed in military issue, other times he wore Vietcong black pajamas. We were never certain if he was VC or an NVA officer. We thought we'd killed him a dozen times. Twice we brought back bodies we were positive were him. But a week or a month later, we'd get a report he was operating in another sector. I'll never forget that vicious face as long as I live."

"Then when you say you killed him, you can't confirm his death," Smith suggested. "This could be the same man."

"No," said Remo dully, touching the photo with his fingertips as if doubting its solidity. "I killed him. I was three months from rotating stateside. I was walking point on a six-man patrol. Youngblood was there then. Yeah. We'd received word of VC activity in what had been a friendly village. Youngblood led us in. We found nothing in the huts. But one of the guys, Webb—from Iowa, I think—shoved his rifle barrel into a garbage pile, checking for hidden supplies. He found a grass mat. Webb lifted it, thinking it was the lid of a spider hole. His face was shot into meat."

Remo's eyes took on a faraway, inward light. He was no longer looking at the photo, though it was right in front of his eyes. He was looking into himself. Smith and Chiun glanced at one another worriedly.

"It wasn't just a spider hole," Remo went on. "It was a VC tunnel. We pumped rounds into it without effect. I volunteered to go into the hole. A blond kid named Ashton went in with me. We threw down a canister of Foo gas first, let it burn off before going down. It was my first time in a tunnel. I was scared, trying not to let it show. Ashton and I worked our way along, using our flashlights. Ashton must have tripped a wire or something. His arm slammed into my face. When I picked myself up, I saw that it wasn't attached to his shoulder anymore. Ashton was all around me. Ashton was everywhere. But I was okay. I fired down the tunnel. I kept firing as I went deeper. I wanted to pay back whoever was down there."

Remo stopped talking. A long silence hung in the air. When he resumed his story, Remo's voice was tiny.

"I had my flashlight in one hand, my M-16 in the other. I shone and shot, shone and shot. I found supplies, food, ammo. But no VC. Then I ran out of tunnel. It just ended. No escape hatch, no people. It was then I knew I was deep in it. I'd seen no branch tunnels along the way. There was no way anyone could have gotten past me. I crouched down, sweating like a pig, and shut off my light to conserve the battery. The air smelled like earthworms. I don't know how long I waited. I didn't know what I was waiting for. I was just getting my courage up when I heard footsteps.

"I jumped up, turned on the light, but the tunnel twisted so much I couldn't see around the bend. I set my light in the dirt so I could see whatever was coming. I gripped my M16 so hard my hands ached. I was going to zap whoever came around the corner. The footsteps came closer and closer. I was scared. I'd been in-country nine months and thought I'd gotten over being scared. But I was scared. Christ, I was only nineteen. I was just a kid."

"It was a terrible war," Smith said sympathetically.

Remo went on as if he hadn't heard.

"I saw the toe of a boot step into the light. I froze. The boot stopped. I didn't know what to do. If it was a VC he would have been wearing rubber sandals. But it might be an NVA regular. I hesitated. I knew whoever was on the other side was hesitating too. My light was shining right where he had to step. I remember I kept flipping my fire-selector switch back and forth, back and forth. I knew my only chance was to shoot first. I'd have no time to hesitate. But I had no way of knowing if the boot belonged to an enemy or a friendly. If he was friendly, I would be better off on single shot. That way, if I did shoot, I might not kill him. But if he was VC or NVA, my only hope would be to cut loose on full automatic. Otherwise I'd take return fire for sure. So I kept switching back and forth, back and forth.

"I remember deciding I should take a chance. I was going to say something. Something dumb like "Who's there?" I never got the chance. The guy jumped. I squeezed my trigger. I was on single shot. Good thing, too. It was Youngblood. I only grazed him. But he opened up on me. I stumbled back in shock.

"I thought it was an earthquake at first. The dirt under my feet went soft, and boom! I jumped to one side, not knowing what was happening. Right into the wall. The tunnel gook had dug himself into the soft red earth and just lay there, breathing through a straw, buried with his weapon across his chest. Then I realized what was happening. Youngblood wasn't shooting at me. He was trying to get the gook. I opened up on him too. I went on full automatic. I emptied my clip into him.

"I'll never forget his face, all covered with dirt, and dead except for these two black eyes that were more alive than any eyes I'd ever seen. We kept pumping rounds at him, but he wouldn't go down. Blood was gushing out of him like he was a fountain. He was a zombie, what we used to call walking wounded. He was dead, but didn't know it. My rifle ran empty. He came toward me like Frankenstein with an AK-47. He was trying to pull the trigger, but he didn't have the strength. Then Youngblood yanked me around the bend and tossed a grenade in his face."

Remo's eyes refocused on the photo of Captain Dai.

"When the dirt finally settled, we went back to check the body, but the tunnel had caved in. When we got out into the air, Youngblood said, 'We got him, man! We got him!'

"I said, 'Who?' I was starting to tremble all over. I wasn't focusing. 'Didn't you recognize him?' he asked me. 'Captain Spook. That there was Captain Spook. And he's really dead this time.' Those were the exact words he used," Remo said, looking up at Smith and Chiun. " 'He's really dead this time.' "

Smith looked at Remo with something like pity in his eyes. At length he said, "Whoever he is—" Smith's voice disintegrated into a phlegmy grumble. He cleared his throat and started over. "Whoever he was, he's dead. The man who killed Phong is not. If he hasn't left the country already, we'll get him."

"No, you won't," Remo said. "He's a ghost. You can't find him, and even if you did, you wouldn't be able to do anything to him because he's already dead."

"Er, I will leave you with Chiun for now. I'm sure he is anxious to resume your training."

Remo said nothing.

Pausing at the door, Smith said, "I hope we can count on your cooperation, Remo."

"Why shouldn't you?"

"It's just that if you do decide to go to Vietnam on your own and you succeed in freeing your friend, it will be my responsibility, purely for national-security reasons, to see that he doesn't live to tell the world that Remo Williams is not dead."

"Sure," Remo said. "Send a kid over to fight for his country, leave him there, and if he gets out, kill him in the name of national security."

"It's not like that and you know it, Remo. We'll get Youngblood and the others out. Our way. The safe way. No one will have to die. Trust us."

"I trusted people like you when they said we were in Vietnam to win."

"History, Remo."

"Maybe, but it's my history. We should never have pulled out of Vietnam. We should have stayed and finished the job. We could have won. We should have won. Look at all the Vietnamese and Cambodians who've died because we let those butchers overrun Southeast Asia. Millions. Millions."

"That's another conversation. Let me know how he progresses," Smith told Chiun. "Good-bye, Remo."

The door closed gently.

"We should have won," Remo repeated. "We could have beat them."

"The French said the same thing," Chiun said, standing over Remo with his hands folded. "And the Japanese before them and the Chinese before them, and before them, others. You cannot beat the Vietnamese. No one has ever beaten the Vietnamese."

"Don't lecture me about the Vietnamese. I fought them. They weren't so hot."

"Agreed," Chiun said. "They won because they cheated. They do not fight like soldiers. They ambush and shoot. Then they run away. They are incapable of fighting fair. So they resort to murder and skulk in the night. It is nothing new. They have been doing this for centuries. The Vietnamese are always at war. For thousands of years. In the entire history of Sinanju, only two Masters have ever worked for Vietnam. This was back in the days of the Ammamese kings. I think Vietnam gave us work for two months in 12 B.C. and again for a week three centuries later. The rest of the time, they have been fighting neighboring countries."

"You'd think they'd get sick of it."

"No. War is their only industry. They are always fighting because they have nothing else, no art, no culture, no talents. They can barely grow rice."

"We could have won," Remo said stubbornly.

"No, you could never have won. You might have beat

the Vietnamese of the North on your own, but you were handicapped."

"Yeah, by the brass hats who wouldn't go all the way."

"No, by your allies, the Vietnamese of the South. You expected them to fight with you. You expected them to defend themselves. Instead, they hid behind the uniforms of this country and let the bullets intended for them bury themselves in American bodies. Instead of defending the South, you should have taken the South Vietnamese and dropped them into the North by airplane with instructions to murder and rape at will. The war would have been over in a month, the Americans could have gone home, and the ruling Vietnamese could have found themselves other victims to kill. But because you expected the South Vietnamese to fight like soldiers, you lost. It is not in their nature."

Remo grunted. "We used to have this joke. The only way to end the war would be to put the friendly Vietnamese on boats and bomb the whole country flat. Then torpedo the boats."

"It would have been a waste of good boats," Chiun said.

Remo stood up. "I don't agree with you, Chiun. Not all Vietnamese were like that. I knew some I respected. I knew some brave ones. And there was Phong."

"You did not know him."

"I know the kind of man he was. He risked his life to come to America to tell the truth about American MIA's."

Chiun spat on the floor. "He only wanted to come to America. Everyone wants to come to America."

"He didn't have to go on TV. He knew he was being stalked. He wanted to help his friends, my friends."

"Enough," said Chiun, slapping his hands. "We can discuss this later. First, we train."

Remo stopped to pick up the crumpled ball of paper. "You really zapped me with this old trick?"

"Your mind was not on your center. It is my job to realign your essence with the universe."

"How can you do that when I feel the world spinning under me?"

"That is a temporary backflash."

"You know," Remo said dreamily, "I haven't felt right since Mah-Li died. Everything seems to have fallen apart. The woman I almost married died. I find out I have a daughter I didn't even know about, but because of the work I do, her mother is raising her alone. I don't even know where they are. All my life I've been looking forward to turning the corner to a normal existence. But now I feel like all the good days are in the past. Like the key to my happiness lies in the past."

"It does," Chiun said. "It lies in your early training, which I will now attempt to duplicate, although I am not as young as I once was."

Remo smiled bitterly. "Can we start with bullet-dodging?"

"If you wish. Why?"

"Because I think it's been my turn for about fifteen years."

9

It was the end of a long day and Harold Smith was weary. He left his office feeling his age. Smith was about to enter his car when he noticed that the Folcroft gymnasium lights were still on. It'd been a week since Remo Williams had been brought back for retraining, and Smith was still worried about him. He shut the car door and, even though he intended to be gone only a minute or two, took along his ever-present briefcase. He walked up the flagstone path to the gymnasium door.

Smith found Remo and the Master of Sinanju in the spacious exercise area. Remo was standing at one end of the long court, one leg slightly ahead of the other, his body strained forward like a sprinter about to go. Chiun stood off to one side, his hands bristling with ornamental daggers.

At the sound of Smith's approach, Chiun turned. He beamed happily.

"Greetings, Emperor Smith. You are just in time to see Remo ascend the dragon."

"I'm not familiar with that maneuver," Smith admitted.

"Oh, it is quite simple. Remo will run from one end of the room to the other while I throw these daggers at him as accurately as possible."

"Those are rubber daggers, I trust."

"Of course not. If they were rubber, Remo would know they were rubber and not even try to avoid them. They are real."

"Can Remo handle this so soon?" Smith wondered.

"We will find out. He has progressed reasonably."

"I guess this won't be too difficult for a man who can sidestep bullets."

"Ah, but the dagger-avoiding is not the true test."

"No?" Smith shifted his briefcase from one hand to the other. It never occurred to him to set it down.

"Remo must return to his starting place without his feet touching the floor," Chiun explained.

"I don't understand."

"Watch," Chiun raised his voice. "Remo, show Smith your recovering prowess."

Remo flashed along the varnished pinewood floor. He was a blur whose legs floated as they moved. The backwash as he passed disturbed Smith's sparse white hair and sent his Dartmouth tie fluttering. Smith grabbed the tie to keep it from slapping his face.

"Any word on the AIM's?" Chiun asked. He made no move to throw the daggers.

"MIA's. No. In fact, there has been a minor setback. The Vietnamese have toughened their position. They want some economic sanctions lifted as a good-faith gesture before the hard bargaining begins. It's starting to become a replay of the Paris peace talks. It could drag on into next year."

"No need to tell Remo."

"I agree. Aren't you going to throw those knives?"

"Soon, soon," said Chiun, glancing at Remo's hurtling form.

"And shouldn't Remo slow down? He's going to hit that wall."

Remo did hit the wall. And kept on going. His feet flashed ahead of him, and suddenly he was running up the wall, carried by sheer momentum. He was literally running against gravity.

"How high can he go?" Smith asked.

"To the moon, if you had such a wall," Chiun said blandly.

"Come now," Smith scoffed.

Then Smith's thin mouth puckered like the frame for a life-saver. Remo was running along the ceiling. Running upside down.

Chiun's hands went to work. In a series of overhand flips he sent the daggers away. They streaked toward the ceiling. He folded his empty hands into his voluminous sleeves.

Remo, seeming to float like a runner in a weightless environment, began to zigzag across the ceiling. Daggers sprouted around his feet. None hit him. He neared the opposite wall.

"This is the most difficult step of all," Chiun confided.

"I would think it would be the easiest. All he has to do is jump."

"No. Jumping is not allowed. Remo is now running against gravity. In the opposite direction. When he reaches the wall, he must run into the direction of gravity, but not so fast that he does fall. He has ascended the dragon. Now he must descend the dragon."

"From a physics standpoint, I don't think this is possible."

"For American physics, perhaps not. This is Korean physics."

Remo hit the wall. This time, he seemed to backflip into place. He was halfway down before he began to skid.

Remo flailed about for a minute and gave up. He twisted like a cat, landing on both feet. He hit without a sound.

Smith started to applaud. "Very good! Bravo, bravo!"

The Master of Sinanju turned to him with blazing hazel eyes. He forced Smith's hands apart. "Are you mad? He has bumbled this simple exercise and you give him a reward. How will he relearn perfection if he is applauded for failure? Worse, when he does succeed, he will expect greater rewards. I am training an assassin, not a performing dog."

"Sorry."

Chiun folded his arms imperiously and bestowed upon Remo a cold, agatelike stare. Remo walked up dejectedly.

"I think I lost my concentration at the end," he admitted.

"Obviously," Chiun said, his voice dripping disappointment. "And in front of Emperor Smith. Smith is very angry with you. He just now explained to me that he may offer me a new pupil, the eldest son of the President. I am considering his offer. I could work with a younger student, one with fewer ingrained habits. A young pupil would not shame me as you just did."

"If I did so badly, who was that applauding just now?" Remo asked.

"Applause? I heard no applause. Did you hear any such noise, Emperor?"

Smith looked uncomfortable. "Ah . . ."

"I heard it distinctly," Remo insisted.

"You must be referring to the sound of your emperor's feet stamping in frustration and anger," Chiun informed him coldly. "That is the only sound you heard—the only sound you deserve."

"Thanks a bunch. Any word on those negotiations, Smitty?"

"Um, nothing has changed. There has been progress, but not real change."

"You know, Smitty, if you're going to lie like that, you should try to get better at it."

"Yes, well . . . how are you feeling?"

"Like my old self," Remo said, rotating his thick wrists impatiently.

"You're sounding like your old self too."

"Do not be fooled, Emperor Smith. He still sometimes babbles about how the war was unfair to him and if he could only go back, he would have won it. All by himself. He sounds like that film creature, Dumbo."

"The flying elephant?" Smith asked.

"I think he means Rambo," Remo said hastily. "And I was not babbling, just making conversation. Honest."

"I see," said Smith.

"In fact," Remo said airily, "I feel so much better, I think I'll go for a walk, if that's all right with everybody. I've been cooped up in this gym too long. I need fresh air."

"What do you think, Master of Sinanju?" Smith asked good-naturedly.

"I think fresh air would be good for Remo."

"Fine. Thanks," Remo said, heading for the door.

"You're not thinking of anything foolish, are you, Remo?"

Remo turned, his hand gripping the doorknob. He smiled tightly and asked, "Who, me?" His face was open and innocent, like a child's.

"Because if you are, you should be aware that I've revoked every credit card under each of your cover identities."

"Appreciate the vote of confidence, Smitty." Remo's face was still frozen in an icy, ingratiating smile.

"Nothing personal. Just a precaution."

"Do not worry, Emperor," Chiun said expansively. "Remo may sometimes appear foolish, but only Remo. I am not foolish. And I am going nowhere, especially to Vietnam. And Remo thinks too much of his trainer to bring humiliation upon his name. And I say to you now that I give you my word as a Master of Sinanju that Remo will not leave this country except by your leave. Is that not so, Remo?"

"Chiun speaks for both of us," Remo agreed, his knuckles whitening on the doorknob. "What better guarantee could you ask for?"

"I am relieved to hear that. Have a good time, Remo."

"The best." And Remo was out the door like it had swallowed him.

* * *

Remo walked the dark streets of Rye, New York, with his hands in his pockets. The night was cold, but he didn't feel it. The wind rippled his black T-shirt and chinos, but inside he was warm.

And angry.

"Damn Smith for canceling my credit cards," he muttered to himself. That left him without an easy first step. He wondered how he was going to get out of the country, never mind all the way to Vietnam, without money. He wondered how far he could get on foot. Phong had gotten out of Vietnam on foot, and Phong was not Remo. Lately, even Remo hadn't been Remo. But after a week under Chiun's hard tutelage, he felt up to the job. And he had fooled both Chiun and Smith into thinking he had abandoned his plans.

Remo was pondering his problem when a voice growled at him from a shadowy doorway.

"Take 'em out of the pockets, friend," it warned.

Remo saw a gleaming barrel of a chrome-plated .357 Magnum revolver aimed at him. He considered ignoring the man, when a better thought occurred to him.

Remo stopped in his tracks. Slowly he took his hands out of his pockets and turned to face the man in the darkened doorway.

"Easy," Remo said, a catch in his voice. "I don't want any trouble."

"Well, ain't that too damn bad." The man sneered, stepping into the light. "Because you sure got it. Now, fork over your wallet."

"Please, mister, don't shoot me," Remo pleaded.

The man inched closer. His breath, like sour milk, wafted into Remo's face. "The wallet," he repeated.

The man was close enough now. Remo's foot lashed out and made contact with a kneecap. The gunman screamed as a kaleidoscope of pain-induced lights exploded behind his eyes. His kneecap felt like a fragmenting grenade. His arm flew up and struck the wall behind him. When he tried to yank it down, it wouldn't pull free.

"I said I didn't want trouble," Remo told him in a grating voice. "I didn't say I don't like trouble, because I do. I didn't mean I can't handle trouble, because as you'll plainly notice, your knee is broken and your gun is embedded six inches into a brick wall with your hand still wrapped around it. What I meant was, I wasn't in the mood for trouble. But now that I don't have a choice, I plan to make the best of it."

The gunman looked at the brick wall above his head. He saw that his leather-jacket cuff was touching brick. He pulled it back and there was his wrist, and then there was the brick. There was no sign of his hand. The wall wasn't shattered or cracked. Not even the mortar was disturbed. It looked as if the wall had grown around his hand. He felt the trigger under his finger and decided against pulling it. No telling what might happen.

Instead, he looked into the dead, flat eyes of the skinny guy who had done this to him. He decided an apology was in order.

"I apologize," he said sincerely.

"Too late. My night is ruined. You're going to have to make it up to me."

"How? Just tell me. I'll do it."

"I need some fast cash."

"Left-front pants pocket. Help yourself. Just leave me bus fare, okay?"

"Thank you," said Remo. He extracted the man's wallet. It was fat and black. Remo riffled through it. He counted out nearly thirteen hundred dollars in wrinkled bills.

"What were you sticking me up for?" Remo demanded of the would-be holdup man. "You got a small fortune here."

"How do you think I come to be carrying that large a wad? Working as a hairdresser?"

"Well, you're donating it to a new fund. The Free the U.S. POW's Fund. It so happens I'm president and treasurer."

"I'm a charitable man. Easy come, easy go."

"I can use this credit card too," Remo said, stuffing the wallet back into the man's dungaree pocket.

The gunman scowled. "Hey, have a heart, man. That ain't fair. That's my own credit card. I didn't steal it. You can have the money, okay? I can always steal more. But getting square with the credit-card people, that's real work."

"Think of yourself as Robin Hood. You're stealing from the rich and giving it to the poor. Me."

"This ain't fair."

"No, it ain't," Remo admitted, starting off. "Toodle-oo."

"Hey! What am I gonna do about my hand? It's still caught in this wall."

Remo turned. "You still have your own teeth?" he asked.

"Yeah. So?"

"Start gnawing brick."

The woman at the travel agency was a crisp, no-nonsense blond in a black-and-white business suit set off with a string tie. Remo decided he liked the way a lock of her hair fell over her smooth brow. She had the shiniest ears he'd ever seen. Remo wondered why it was that blonds always had ears that looked as if they were waxed daily.

"And where would your travel plans be taking you?" she asked.

Remo hesitated. He decided to trust her. He leaned closer and let her get the full impact of his magnetic charm.

"Between you and me, how close can you get me to Vietnam?"

She leaned into Remo's face conspiratorially. "Hanoi or Ho Chi Minh City?" she asked breathily.

"You can do that?" Remo asked, taken aback.

"Uh-huh," she said. "We have a package plan. It's called the TransVietnam tour. Vietnam is hungry for tourist dollars. Of course, there are no direct flights from this country."

"Of course," Remo said, blinking. This seemed almost too easy.

"But we can book you to Bangkok, Thailand, where you can pick up a connecting flight. It's a two-week tour and includes all meals and hotels."

"I'll be brown-bagging," Remo said. "I've eaten Vietnamese before."

"Oh, were you there? During the war, I mean?"

"Does it show that much?" Remo asked.

"Not on you. You look kinda young, actually—now that I think of it. But this tour is very popular with servicemen. Nostalgia, you know."

"Nostalgia is a terrible thing," Remo said, thinking of his year in Nam.

"So—Hanoi or Ho Chi Minh City?"

"Ho Chi Minh City—that used to be Saigon, right?"

"Um-huh." The blond was wetting her lips with her tongue.

"I'll take it."

"When would you like to depart?" she asked, calling up a schedule on her desk terminal.

"When's the next flight?"

"Well, there's one tonight, but obviously—"

"I'll take it," Remo said quickly.

"You'll need a connecting flight to Kennedy International."

"First class," Remo said. "All the way. A friend is paying for it."

The blond lifted penciled eyebrows quizzically and got to work.

"How do you plan to pay for this?" she asked.

"Credit card," Remo said, placing one on the desk like a bridge player laying down his trump.

The blond picked it up and began entering the information on her terminal. A minute later, she presented Remo with a sheaf of airline tickets.

"There you are, Mr. Krankowski. Is that how you pronounce it?"

" 'Krankowski' is fine," he said, pocketing his receipt. The blond had forgotten to verify his signature, which was a break.

"Well, if you expect to make your nine o'clock flight, I suggest you get going. Too bad, though. I was kinda hoping we'd have a drink. I'm about to close."

Remo stood up to go. "Another time. For sure."

"Oh, don't forget your credit card, Michael. Do they call you Mickey or Mike?"

"Remo."

Her eyebrows shot up. "Remo?"

"It's my stage name," Remo explained. "Remo the Awesome. I'm a professional magician. I've toured every continent."

"Oh," said the blond, cupping her chin in one hand and smiling warmly. "And just what sort of magic is it that you do?"

"At the moment, I'm working on my disappearing act."

10

Saigon had changed in more than name.

Remo had checked into his room at the Thong Nhat, one of the few presentable hotels in what was now called Ho Chi Minh City. Because he had no baggage, Remo couldn't change clothes. He plopped down on the bed and turned on the suite's Vietronics TV. There were two channels. On one, a jagged-voiced woman with severe hair droned on while scenes of hardworking peasants flashed on a graphic insert beside her head. Remo's Vietnamese wasn't up to following the thread of the talk. The other channel showed a cartoon. A pack of mice in black pajamas harassed a band of GI cats waving a tattered American flag. The mice were winning.

Remo snapped off the TV and shoved up the window. He leaned out. Whatever they called it now, Saigon still smelled like New York's Chinatown. Once, the city streets had been clogged with little cars and military vehicles. Now everyone rode bicycles. Remo saw only one car in twenty minutes of watching. And only two Honda motor scooters, which had once been so plentiful. Whatever Communist rule had brought to the South, prosperity was not part of the package.

There was a little service-bar refrigerator in one corner. Remo opened it up. It was stocked with sick-looking water in bottles, several bottles of Viet Min beer, and cans of a soft drink that said, in English and Vietnamese, "Melon Grass Drink."

Remo decided the water was his best bet. He was wrong. He took one mouthful and spit it into the bathroom sink.

"Well, maybe it will rain," he muttered hopefully.

The telephone buzzed raucously.

"Mr. Krankowski?" The desk clerk mangled the name all out of shape. Remo said yes.

"Tour group leaving in ten minutes."

"You people don't give tourists much time to settle in."

"Tour group on very strict schedule. Please be in lobby in ten minutes."

"Okay," Remo said, hanging up. He looked at the TransVietnam tour booklet. It included chaperoned tours of portions of the Ho Chi Minh Trail, and as a capper, three luxurious days in Hanoi, the former North Vietnamese capital. Remo didn't expect to ever see Hanoi. He planned to leave the tour group when he got as close to Cambodia as he could get. He left the room.

The tour group was composed of several Russians, an East German couple, and a thick-set man who said he was from North Carolina.

The North Carolinian sidled up to Remo nervously.

"Sure glad to see another American on this trip, friend."

"Same here," Remo said noncommittally. He decided not to get too friendly with the man. It would only complicate things.

"Stick with me, friend, and I'll tell you about the war. I was here in those days. I was a REMF, myself. I'll bet you can't guess what that means."

"It means rear-echelon-motherfucker," Remo said flatly. "I was in Nam too."

"You pulling my leg? You couldn't have been. Not unless the Army was drafting eight-year-olds."

"I was a Marine. First Battalion, Twenty-sixth Marines."

"No kidding?"

"No kidding," Remo said.

"You look, what—twenty-eight?"

"What I look like and what I am are two different things."

"I'll take your word for it. Hey, this looks like the bus. Did they paint it that color, or is that jungle rot?"

Remo didn't answer as he climbed into the bus. He made a point of taking a seat next to one that was without a cushion. The North Carolinian frowned, but took the hint. He sat in the back and the bus rattled down potholed streets and past the gates of the old Doc Lap Palace and then north. Remo stared out the window in thought. He was surprised that he'd revealed the military background to the other American. But the words had just slipped out. Remo had once been so proud of the Corps. But all that had happened to him since Vietnam made everything that had gone before insignificant—like comparing the gold star you got in the third grade with a Congressional Medal of Honor.

The road turned to dirt and the last houses gave way to sugarcane fields. A chubby tour guide turned in his seat behind the driver. He picked up a microphone and introduced himself as Mr. Hom. Then he began his talk, speaking alternately in German, Russian, and English. It was the same speech in each language, about how the peoples of North and South Vietnam had been finally reunited after years of forced separation by the imperialist Americans. Remo tuned the man out and thought about his old life. A passing flash of elephant grass made his stomach clench involuntarily. Fear. He had not felt fear in a long time. Fear meant his training had not completely reasserted itself. Remo wondered if maybe he had left America too soon.

As Mr. Hom droned on, Remo felt the years melt away, back to 1968. And suddenly a thought occurred to him—a simple thought. He had always thought of his life as divided into two parts. Each was separate—almost as if he'd been two people sharing the same memories. His old life had ended when he was arrested for a crime he didn't commit and sentenced to the electric chair. It'd been a frame, with Dr. Harold W. Smith the framer. Thus had Remo Williams, former Newark cop, been drafted into service for CURE.

All that happened before had belonged to a previous life. There was only one link. A CIA agent named Conn MacCleary, whom Remo had encountered in Vietnam. Remo had single-handedly executed a critical mission under MacCleary's orders, a mission that should have required a battalion: storming a farmhouse and getting important security papers before the VC could burn them.

MacCleary—now dead—later went to work for Harold Smith. And when CURE required a one-man army to do its work, MacCleary had remembered an intense marine named Remo Williams.

Yes, Remo thought sleepily. That was the link. In a way, it had all started in Vietnam. And now he was back. The heat filled the lumbering bus. The tour guide babbled on about Vietnam's internationalist responsibility, and outside insects droned. Somehow their drone made more sense. Remo dozed off.

Hours later, the motor changed tune and the bus jounced as it left the road. Remo blinked awake. He was surprised at how sluggish he felt. Maybe it was the heat. Then he remembered, as if over a long span of years, that he was a Master of Sinanju. He could walk naked across the Sahara or the South Pole in serene comfort.

"Welcome to People's Reeducation Camp Forty-seven," Mr. Hom said. "We will now show you the good things we have done with those of the puppet South who were corrupted by capitalism."

Remo made a face. He had Hom pegged as a low-level Communist-party political officer. But he decided to ignore the man, no matter how rankling his words. When Remo slipped away from the tour group, he didn't want to be conspicuous by his absence.

The camp consisted of a four-sided chain-link fence surrounding long, barrackslike, unpainted buildings. A Vietnamese flag flew from a pole, its yellow star fluttering against a blood-red background.

"Follow me, please," Mr. Hom instructed. His English was good, if mushily enunciated.

Remo hung back in the rear of the group. The bus had stopped at the gate, which was opened by two pith-helmeted armed guards. The group was escorted into the perimeter. There were no guard towers, no barbed wire. It was obviously a minimum-security installation. Remo wondered if the POW camp he sought would be this easy to penetrate. Probably not. This had to be a showcase to impress foreign visitors.

Mr. Hom continued to talk as he waddled along. He spoke into a hand-held mike that hooked up to a portable speaker he carried slung over his shoulder—as if he couldn't trust anyone to listen to him unless his decibel level was set at excruciating.

"When the glorious People's Army liberated Ho Chi Minh City," he explained, "many Southerners had been under Western influence too long. They were lazy and indolent. They had absorbed American propaganda. They would not work. In our kindness, we brought them here, to teach them to work."

Looking at Mr. Hom's wide, unlined face, Remo decided that that had happened while Hom was in diapers. But the man went on as if he'd personally executed the policy.

Mr. Hom led them to one of the barracks and up its rough wood steps. Inside, there were Vietnamese people sitting together at long tables. Some wove baskets. Other appeared to be making sandals out of old truck tires. They looked up as the tour group crowded inside, their eyes sad and empty.

"Many of these were criminals and prostitutes before," Mr. Hom explained, turning the sound down because it echoed in the close confines. "Every day, they rise early, attend indoctrination lessons, and work at simple tasks. Soon they will be rehabilitated."

Remo, comparing the intelligent expressions of the Vietnamese captives with the dull faces of the soldiers and Mr. Hom's flabby, stupid expression, couldn't resist making a remark.

"Saigon was overrun in 1975, more than ten years ago. Why are these people still here?"

Mr. Hom turned on the group, searching each face with beady eyes. "Who speaks? You, American?"

"Yes," Remo said levelly. "I am an American."

"Your question is impertinent. But I will answer for the benefit of the others. These are stubborn cases. They are not ready to enter socialist society. Here, they are useful, to the state and to themselves."

"They look like political prisoners—or prisoners of war."

"They have been liberated. A less-enlightened regime might have had them executed."

"Yeah," Remo said, an edge to his voice. "You're too enlightened to hold POW's. Of *any* kind."

"Yes, exactly," said Mr. Hom, thinking that Remo was agreeing with him. He turned to the rest of the tour group, satisfied in his mind that the dark-eyed American had been put in his place. He repeated his answer in German. Then again in Russian. The Russians nodded in agreement.

Remo slid around the knot of tourists and edged close to one of the tables. A middle-aged woman with graying hair pulled back in a bun was weaving a basket. Remo whispered to her, "Do you speak English?"

The woman nodded slightly, not taking her eyes off her work.

"What did you do before the war?"

"I was a teacher," she said. Her words were more breath than bite, but Remo understood them.

"And you?" Remo asked a man with tortoiseshell glasses.

"Engineer."

"Any message you want me to carry back to the world?"

"Yes. Tell the Americans to come back." The woman nodded in agreement. Others did too.

One of the guards noticed Remo and stepped forward. He slapped the old woman. Remo slapped him back. The soldier went in one direction, his rifle in another. His helmet clanged off a wall, sounding like an old gong.

"What is this?" Mr. Hom's cry was shrill.

"This enlightened Communist slapped that old woman without reason," Remo pointed out.

"Lies! Vietnamese only strike women for politically correct reasons. What are you doing there, American? Return to the group. There is no talking to internees here."

"Why don't I wait outside?" Remo suggested.

Mr. Hom stiffened. He looked from Remo to the others in the group, and evidently remembering the image he wished to project of the new Vietnam, nodded sullenly.

"Wait on the steps. We will join you almost at once."

"Don't hurry on my account," Remo said, pointedly stepping on the prostrate soldier's stomach on his way to the door.

Outside, he watched the sun setting over a bushy ridge. He rubbed his eyes. They were caked with dried fluid. He felt tired, and wondered if it was jet lag. But jet lag was something he had banished from his life long ago.

Remo noticed the next barracks were unguarded. He drifted over and put an ear to the door. He heard breathing and low talking. Finding a sealed window, he looked in.

Looking out at him was a man with blue eyes and Caucasian features. His face exploded in shock at the sight of Remo's face.

"American, American!" he shouted in English. "You come to rescue?"

"Damn right," said Remo, taking the wooden frame in his hands. He yanked. The sash came off like a picture frame.

Remo helped the man out. He wore black pajamas, the traditional Vietnamese peasant clothes. His hair was black, like a Vietnamese's. But his face was white.

"Where helicopters?" His accent was pure Vietnamese.

"What helicopters?" Remo asked.

"Liberation helicopters. You American. You come to liberate Vietnam?"

"Not exactly," said Remo, noticing two more faces poking out the window. One was Vietnamese, but his skin was milk chocolate. Another was a girl. Her skin was Asian, but her face was freckled, her large eyes green as an Irish colleen's.

"How many of you are there?" Remo asked.

"Twenty."

"You're not POW's, I take it," Remo said.

"Yes. Prisoner long time."

"Not American POW's," Remo said disappointedly, as the others began to climb out the window, chattering excitedly and clinging to one another in fear. Remo looked around. So far, no guards in sight. But that wouldn't last long with the noise they were making.

The first man was talking excitedly and grabbing Remo's T-shirt.

"Yes."

"Yes, what?" Remo demanded.

"Yes, American. Half."

"Half?" Then the tour group spilled out of the other building. Mr. Hom saw Remo and shouted in Vietnamese. Guards came running raggedly, looking around in confusion.

Hom pointed to Remo and the hole in the barracks, out of which teenage prisoners were now pouring, dressed in rags. The guards, who looked out of practice, got organized.

Mr. Hom waddled up to Remo, flanked by the soldiers. They held their rifles at the ready. Hom flapped his arms like a pelican trying to fly.

"You break camp rules," he screeched. "You break camp rules. This is nasty. You are not to see those people. What is the meaning?"

"I thought I was liberating American POW's," Remo said stubbornly.

That upset Hom even more. "There are no American POW's in Vietnam," he yelled. "We are not like that. Though you bomb us, we forgave you. These are *bui doi*, dust of life. What you call Amerasians. They are the mongrel children of Saigon prostitutes and American killer soldiers."

"They say they're prisoners," Remo said. The young captives crouched behind him. The girl, her green eyes fearful, clung to Remo's T-shirt. She looked all of nineteen. Her face had the look of a jib that had been cranked too tight.

"Lies! They are here because no one wants them. We feed them, give them work. They are grateful."

"Take us home, American," the prisoners whispered. "Take us to America."

"I think that speaks for itself," Remo pointed out. He folded his arms, ignoring the pointing rifles.

"You are very smug, American," said Mr. Hom. "You

spit on the generous hospitality of the Vietnamese people. I think you should return to America. You will
learn nothing here."

"I didn't come here to learn your propaganda," Remo
said. "And I'm not budging until I know these people
won't be hurt."

Mr. Hom hesitated. He felt the eyes of the tour
group upon him. His next words dripped sarcasm.

"Perhaps you are still bitter about having retreated
from the victorious People's Liberation Army. Hmmm?"

"We didn't retreat, remember?" Remo said. "We
signed a peace treaty in Paris. Your people promised to
stay in the North and ours in the South. It took you
about a year to muster the courage to violate it."

"We liberated the South," Hom said stiffly.

"You couldn't win on the battlefield, so you tricked
us with a treaty you never intended to uphold. Then
you stabbed everyone in the back."

"We won."

"Maybe it's not over yet," Remo said. His voice held
an edge that made Mr. Hom wipe suddenly sweaty
palms on his whipcord breeches.

Mr. Hom barked orders in Vietnamese. The guards
lowered their weapons. Two went around a corner.
They came back driving a Land Rover.

"You will be driven back to Ho Chi Minh City," Mr.
Hom said petulantly. "There your money will be re-
funded and you will be put on a flight away from
Vietnam. Perhaps one day you will realize the goodness
of the forgiving Vietnamese people and we will allow
you to return."

Remo, knowing he had no chance of doing anything
for the Amerasian prisoners under the circumstances,
shrugged as if it didn't matter. He said, "Okay," and
turned to the huddle of frightened half-Vietnamese,
half-American faces.

"Sorry," he said loudly. Then he whispered, "Sit tight. I'll be back."

Remo allowed himself to be escorted to the waiting Land Rover and driven out of the camp gates. The amplified voice of Mr. Hom followed him down the road. Hom was informing the tour group that in America, many people felt bitterness over their failure to impose their will on the Vietnamese people. But the Vietnamese were strong from thousands of years of struggle. No one would ever divide them again.

11

Less than a mile down the road, darkness fell with the stark suddenness that Remo remembered so clearly even after twenty years.

The soldiers sat in the front of the Land Rover. Remo sat in back. The driver was preoccupied with watching the road ahead. He had only his headlights to see by. Remo reached out and squeezed the other soldier's neck until he felt the man go loose. Remo kept him sitting upright while they stumbled through ruts in the road.

When the driver slowed to negotiate a sharp turn, Remo brought his fist down on his helmet like a mallet striking a bell. The driver collapsed like a puppet. Remo shoved him onto the roadside and slipped behind the wheel. He braked, kicked the other soldier into the dirt, and spun the Land Rover around.

Remo drove until he recognized a diseased banana tree that was near the reeducation camp, and pulled off the road. On foot he crept up to the perimeter fence and went over it like a black cat.

He drifted through the camp, keeping in the shadows. The lethargy of the day had fled. He felt alert once again. Maybe it had been the heat after all.

The tour group was eating in a wooden building, and behind it Remo found several Land Rovers and a canvas-backed truck. Reasoning that the kitchen was at the back of the big building, he slipped to the door. It came open at his touch. Inside, an elderly Vietnamese cook was busy pulling wooden pallets of fresh bread from a huge oven. Remo went to a cupboard and ransacked it. When he left the kitchen unseen, two canvas sacks bulged under his arms.

There was just enough sugar to pour into the gas tank of every vehicle. Remo replaced the gas caps and found his way to the barracks where the Amerasians were kept. A soldier in green was nailing bamboo splints across the broken window. Remo put him to sleep with a single chopping blow and removed the bamboo with quick tugs. He poked his head in.

"Next bus leaves in two minutes," he called. "You can buy your tickets on board."

They poured out of the window like lemmings. Remo helped the younger ones over the sill. When he had them collected in a group, he put his fingers to his mouth to gesture for quiet.

"Now, listen. I can get you out of here and away. But after that, you're on your own. Understand?"

They nodded, their faces pale and grateful.

"Okay," Remo said. "Single file, and follow me. Don't bunch up."

He led them to the next barracks and then to the one nearest the gate. Motioning for them to stay out of sight, Remo slipped to the gate and approached the guard.

Remo was almost up to him when his foot hit a rock. It was the strangest thing. He should have seen the rock. At the very least, he should have sensed it before kicking it. He was trained not to betray himself. But he had.

The guard spun. His Ak-47 hung from a shoulder strap. He brought it up snappily. Remo was quicker. He grabbed the weapon by barrel and stock, and spun like a top. The centrifugal force made the guard let go. The strap held for three revolutions, then snapped. The guard sailed over the fence and crashed into the upper branches of a rubber tree. He lay still.

Remo broke the padlock, kicked the gate open, and waved for the others to come.

They started off single file, but the open gate was too much for them. The orderly escape became a rout.

Still clutching the captured rifle, Remo yanked the external lever that opened the folding bus doors. He slid behind the wheel as the others found seats and huddled under the exposed window glass. In a moment, Remo had hot-wired the ignition and got going.

The sound of the bus rumbling brought excited yells from the camp. Engines started growling, but the engines didn't catch. That would be the sugar. Remo grinned.

In the rearview mirror Remo saw the Vietnamese soldiers pile into the road, some dropping into a shooting crouch, others bringing their rifles to shoulder height.

Mr. Hom, hopping up and down like an animated pelican, slapped their rifle barrels down before they could fire. He swore at them, pointing to the gawking tour group, who were watching the brave soldiers of the new Vietnam trying to organize pursuit without vehicles.

Remo grinned again. It reminded him of the day in September 1967 when he stole a North Vietnamese tank from under the noses of its sleeping crew. He pushed the accelerator to the floor, driving after the setting sun, toward Cambodia.

It was many miles before Remo hit a roadblock.

Two Land Rovers were parked nose-to-nose, blocking the road. About a dozen soldiers were standing in single-file formation in front of the Land Rovers, their rifles high and unwavering. They reminded Remo of paintings of the British Redcoats standing in strict military formation while American guerrillas picked them

off from behind cover. Remo grunted to himself as he
slowed the bus. The Vietnamese were acting like real
soldiers now. That would be their mistake.

Remo barked, "Everybody get on the floor," to his
passengers, yanked the door-opening handle with one
hand, and scooped up his rifle with the other. He
stopped. Noticing the rifle, he asked himself in a dazed
voice, "What the hell am I doing?" Chiun would kill
him if he caught him using a firearm. Remo left the
weapon behind and walked into the bus's headlight
glow with his hands hanging loose and empty.

He smiled as he approached the toylike soldiers.

"Is this the *Road to Mandalay*?" he asked cheerfully.
"Or am I in the wrong movie?"

A dozen safeties clicked off at once.

"Yep," Remo said. "Wrong movie. I want *Tarzan
goes to Vietnam.*"

And without any preliminary tensing of muscle or
other betraying action, Remo vanished from the twin
spray of headlights.

The Vietnamese soldiers blinked. One of them barked
an order. The soldiers advanced into the light, walking
abreast.

Up in the overhanging tree where Remo had disappeared to, he was reminded again of the Redcoats.
Only these soldiers were green. And not just in the
color of their uniforms. Remo found a strong vine,
tested it for weight, and pushed off.

He came down like a pendulum hitting dominoes.
The first soldier never knew what hit him. Neither did
the one next to him, who was thrown into the man
beside him, who in turn clanged helmets with his comrade. The chain reaction of falling soldiers would have
been comical had it not been for the sporadic eruption
of automatic-weapons fire as frantic fingers tightened on
triggers. Rubber-tree leaves were sickled off. Thick tree
boles shattered, spewing milky sap. The Vietnamese
cackled profanity. None of it did them any good.

Once they were tangled up on the road, Remo put the still-conscious ones to sleep with a series of butterfly jabs. He motioned for help, and several Amerasians dragged the soldiers off to the side of the road and confiscated their rifles. Remo had moved the Land Rovers close to the bus and started siphoning gas into jerricans bolted to the back of the bus when the Amerasians wandered out of the dark bush. They were wiping blood stains off confiscated bayonets.

Remo shrugged. War was war.

He finished siphoning off the last of the gas, hurried everyone aboard, and climbed back in.

"Next stop, Cambodia—or whatever they call it now," he announced.

In the back, they giggled nervously. They were quite a mix. American faces with almond eyes. Asian faces with Western eyes. Some were white, some brown, others black. They looked lost.

A rusting road sign told Remo he was on Route Thirteen—what used to be known as the Road to Peace. If memory served, it went directly to the Cambodian border. He settled down for the long haul.

Hours later, a military Land Rover appeared in the rearview mirror and Remo again called for everyone to get onto the floor. They obeyed instantly and yelled, "Go, American!" Remo liked that.

The Land Rover drew abreast like a speedy cockroach and Remo waited until someone in a uniform stood up and shouted for him to pull over.

Remo did. In the Land Rover's direction. The vehicle swerved, precipitating the officer onto the macadam roadway. He rolled several times, his clothes coming off as if he were a shucked ear of corn. The Land Rover spun out of control and piled into a tree.

"Yay, American! Go, GI!" The Amerasians were shouting at the top of their lungs.

They weren't disturbed again until the low *wop-wop-*

wop sound of an approaching helicopter intruded over the engine's rackety roar.

Remo held the wheel while he searched the sky.

"Anybody see a chopper?"

All over the bus, the windows shot up and heads poked out, twisting faces craned to the sky.

The helicopter's *wop-wop-wop* changed to a *whut-whut-whut* and then became a clattering *pocketapocketa* noise, and Remo knew it was closing hard. But from where?

The helicopter—Remo recognized it as a Russian Hind gunship camouflaged green and brown—jumped up from behind a grassy hill and the Amerasians in the right row called that they had spotted it.

"Thanks a lot," Remo muttered. Loudly he said, "Can anyone hit it?"

They tried. AK-47's erupted at the weapons-heavy gunship. It passed overhead, its racket deafening, and vanished from sight.

"Any luck?" Remo called.

"No," someone with a high-pitched voice told him. "We try again."

"Better get it on the next pass because that's when they're going to start shooting," Remo warned.

The Amerasians with weapons piled over to the opposite side of the bus, pushed the others to the floor, and stuck their muzzles into the sky. Remo noticed the freckle-faced young girl lying on her stomach, hands tented, her lips moving silently as she prayed to her ancestors.

Remo listened to the fading helicopter rotors. Then they changed pitch.

"Okay, listen up. It's coming back now. I'm going to hit the brakes. That'll give us a clean shot at them. But they'll have a better shot at us too. Don't blow it."

"Okay," he was told. It was weird to hear Vietnamese voices coming from such American faces.

The gunship was a blot in the night-blue of the sky. It grew, bearing down on them. Remo hit the brakes. The riflemen opened up. They fired sporadically.

"Let them get into range!" Remo warned. "Don't waste ammo."

"We trying!"

"Damn," Remo said. His foot poised over the accelerator. They were sitting ducks, but if he started up, they'd never get that gunship.

Then he noticed the AK-47 he'd set beside the driver's seat. Let Chiun get as upset as he wanted.

Remo hit the door handle as he scooped up the AK-47. He set it for single shot and raised the muzzle sight to eye level. The weapon felt strange and clumsy, like a railroad tie. It'd been so long since he'd used a rifle. He made the gun sight describe slow circles in the air around the looming Hind. He tightened the circle until he could feel the gunship's rotors vibrating the barrel and transmitting the vibration down his arm. Tighter and tighter until he found the center of the gunship. When he could see the pilot's dark glasses clearly, he fired. Once. Then he lowered the rifle confidently.

Nothing happened for several minutes. The others continued to fire raggedly, but Remo knew they wouldn't affect what was about to happen.

The pilot still clutched his stick, but his chin was tilted up. The helicopter started to dance in place. It wobbled, then its tail boom suddenly swung around as the pilot's feet ceased to work the stabilizing rotor pedals.

The gunship reeled, pitched, and suddenly nosed to the earth. It exploded in a spectacular orange fireball. Sooty smoke billowed up after the dissipating flames. The gunship was lost in the smoke. There were screams.

"Okay, let's go!" Remo said, returning to the wheel. He sent the bus careening down the road as his passengers happily congratulated themselves on their combined marksmanship.

Remo rolled his eyes. "This is going to be a long ride," he muttered.

The sun rose on his impassive countenance, and though he welcomed its warmth after the chill of evening, the Master of Sinanju refused to open his hazel eyes.

Harold Smith's footsteps approached, the slightly arthritic creaking of his right knee sounding louder to Chiun than it ever had before. But even for his emperor, the Master of Sinanju did not open his eyes.

"Er, Master of Sinanju?" Smith's voice was hesitant.

"I am awake."

"Good."

"But I have not moved since last we spoke. I have slept all night like this."

"That is your right."

"No," Chiun's parchment lips intoned, "it is my shame, my responsibility, my atonement. But not my right. Never my right."

"Yes," said Smith. He looked at the frail figure of the Master of Sinanju seated on the gravel roof of Folcroft Sanitarium. Chiun wore a thin white kimono, completely without decoration or adornment, the blouse rent so that his hairless chest was bared to the elements. He sat in a lotus position, his tiny feet unshod and his hands held palm-up and loose-fingered in his lap. He faced the rising sun. A chill breeze off nearby Long Island Sound played with the wisps of hair over his ears. His beard hairs danced like wafting smoke.

"I will remain here until my son returns," Chiun said.

"That could be a long time," Smith pointed out.

"If it takes the rest of my life, then so be it. I gave my word that Remo would return and he has not. My word has been violated. Until Remo does return, I will stay here, not eating, not drinking, my flesh exposed to the cruel elements. But I do not worry about the cruelty of the elements. Neither bitter wind nor lashing rain could sting so deep as the indifference of my adopted son, who would allow my promise to be broken."

"Is that your final word?"

"Inviolate word. Absolute word. My word given in Remo's name has been shattered, but the word of a Master of Sinanju, given of his own actions, cannot be broken. Will not be broken," Chiun said emphatically, raising a long-nailed finger. "I have spoken."

"Well," Dr. Smith said unhappily, "I'm not certain I understand, but I won't force you to do anything you feel is dishonorable. I'd just have to find another way to get word to Remo."

Chiun's eyes blazed open. His wrinkles gathered tensely and exploded outward as the impact of Smith's word's hit him.

Chiun was on his feet like a jack-in-the-box springing. Smith recoiled at the unexpected movement. Chiun was suddenly in front of him, looking up into Smith's shocked face.

"Remo. You have word of him?"

"Yes, I do," Smith said shakily. "And it is as I feared."

"He is . . . dead!"

"No, he is in Vietnam."

"Then he might as well be dead," Chiun snapped. "He expressly told us he would not go there."

"It might not be his fault."

"How can he escape that responsibility?" Chiun asked querulously.

"He could be having another flashback. Or something. I don't know. What I do know is that a Rye man named Krankowski has been hospitalized after having his hand removed from a brick wall with jackhammers. This person claims he was mugged by someone fitting Remo's description two night ago. The man has a long criminal record, so I have my own ideas about what really happened. Nevertheless, he claims his credit card was stolen. I ran a check, and someone using that card booked a flight to Bangkok and then on to Ho Chi Minh City on the night we last saw Remo. There's no question in my mind that it was Remo and he is now in Vietnam. God knows what he's doing."

"Perhaps not even Him, knowing Remo," Chiun muttered.

"We can't let Remo run loose over there. He could start an international incident and destroy all chance of getting our POW's back through negotiations."

"I will go there and bring him back," Chiun announced suddenly, the wind flapping his kimono skirts against his bony legs.

"I was hoping you would say that," Smith said gratefully. "But what about your atonement?"

Chiun drew himself up haughtily. "Why should I atone for Remo's idiocy?" he said peevishly. "I will go to Vietnam and drag Remo back by the scruff of his neck. He will sit on this roof without so much as a straw mat under him and atone for his own sins."

"Very good," said Smith, following Chiun to the roof hatch. "I will arrange a flight. There is a U.S. submarine in that area that will take you to a dropoff point. It will be up to you to bring Remo back."

"Remo will come back, never fear."

"Only Remo," Smith said.

Chiun turned. "Not his Army friends?"

Smith hesitated. "Not if any of them know him as Remo Williams. It will be hard on him, but we have no choice. CURE is too important."

"If I have to dispatch one of Remo's friends, he may never forgive me."

"We have no choice. Remo has given us none."

Chiun bowed. "Then the consequences will be on Remo's head, not ours."

12

Remo Williams didn't notice he was running out of gas until the engine started missing. He looked down at the fuel gauge. The red pointer was bouncing off the empty pin.

Remo wrestled the bus over to the shoulder of the highway and braked. He turned in his seat. A score of unblinking eyes looked back at him, like baby owls in a forest.

"Listen up, everyone," Remo told them. "This is just a pit stop. I want everyone who has a rifle to deploy around the bus and stand guard. I hear running water. Probably a stream nearby. Two armed people will escort those who want to drink. Everyone else stay close to the bus. Got that?"

Their exotic faces bobbed in understanding.

"Then let's go," Remo said, jumping out. The AK-47 went over his shoulder without conscious thought.

Remo removed the last remaining jerrican and unscrewed the gas cap. As he poured the evil-smelling gas into the tank, he tried to dig into long-buried memories. He'd been driving all night, and had no idea where he was, or how far it was to the Cambodian border.

One of the Amerasians hovered near him. Remo crooked a finger for him to step into talking range.

"Yes?"

"What's your name, pal?"

"Nguyen."

"How far to the Cambodian border, Nguyen?"

The man scratched his head and stared down the road appraisingly. "Forty kilometers," he said, pointing back in the direction they had come.

"You mean that way," Remo said, emptying the last of the jerrican and nodding in the westerly direction.

Nguyen shook his head.

"No," he insisted, pointing east. "That way."

"That's the road back to Saigon," Remo said. "Cambodia is the other way."

"That road back to Vietnam," the man disagreed. "We in Cambodia now."

Remo dropped the jerrican in surprise. "When did we cross the border?"

"Hour ago. When we pass that mountain."

Remo followed Nguyen's pointing finger. Low on the horizon was a steep, forested summit. Remo had paid it no attention before. Suddenly he recognized it. It was the mountain known as the Black Virgin. It straddled the border of Vietnam and Cambodia. It was many kilometers back.

"Great," Remo said. "Why didn't somebody tell me?"

"No one want you to stop. This dangerous area. Khmer Rouge here. Much fighting."

The others returned from the bush at that moment, some of them wiping cool water off their mouths. They looked refreshed.

Remo went around to the front of the bus, turned on the headlights, and gathered them together in the light.

"This is it, everyone. Cambodia. Last stop. You're on your own now. You have weapons, so you can take care of yourselves."

"You take bus?" asked Nguyen.

"Yes," Remo said. "I'll need it if I'm going to rescue my friend. Sorry."

The green-eyed girl pushed out of the huddled group.

"Please not go, American. Stay with us. Help us reach U.S."

"I wish I could," Remo said sincerely. "But I have a mission."

"We go with you. Help you. Fight fiercely. Not like old ARVN troops. Kill many gook for you."

The others took up her call to action, promising to fight bravely for the American and his friend.

Remo was touched by their willingness to fight by his side, but it was out of the question.

"I work best alone. Next time."

The green-eyed girl came up to Remo, her eyes impossibly sad.

"If I not reach America alive, will you tell my American father I love him?"

"Sure," Remo said. "What's his name?"

"Bob."

"Bob what?"

"Not know other name. You will tell him Lan love him and ask that he will remember me?"

"Yeah, I'll tell him. Bob. Sure. How many green-eyed Bobs can there be in America?"

Lan smiled. Remo forced a smile in return. The poor kid had no idea how big America was.

"Well," Remo said slowly, not really knowing what to say in farewell, "see you all back in America."

The Amerasians waved. They looked too scared to move. For a moment Remo hesitated, wondering if taking them along would possibly work out. They looked so helpless. Even the armed ones. But their very helplessness convinced him they were better off on their own.

Remo tore himself away. He replaced the jerrican in its wire bracket. He checked to make sure the gas cap was on tight. He spent more time at it than necessary, trying to look preoccupied, hoping the others would start walking on their own. But no one took the initiative. They watched him in mute wonderment.

Remo got back behind the wheel. He started the engine. The headlights flared brighter. Then, slowly, he sent the bus lumbering around in a circle. As he passed the huddled group, he shot them a weak salute. They waved back. Remo searched their faces one last time, looking for the girl called Lan. He didn't see her.

Then Remo sent the bus rumbling back toward the border. The Amerasians stood watching him until they were swallowed by the darkening jungle.

Remo felt a slow lump rising in his throat. He tried to swallow it away. It wouldn't go away. He concentrated on the road.

Remo had to guess when he got near the Cambodian border. He used the Black Virgin for a reference point. He remembered having seen a dirt road somewhere along this stretch that veered north. For lack of a better plan, he intended to follow it. He had no idea where the POW camp was. But he knew he would have a better chance of locating it on foot. He hoped to find a place to stash the bus while he conducted his search. He would need the bus later. There was no telling what kind of shape Youngblood and the others would be in.

Remo watched the jungle until he found the road. He slid onto it, and the bus tires started crunching rock. The bus slowed in the dirt. It bounced and rattled.

Remo wondered if the old springs would hold. Then he stopped wondering. Abruptly there was a roaring in his ears and the pressure made his vision turn red, as if the blood vessels in his eyes had all popped at once. He never heard the sound of the explosion.

When Remo woke up, the first thing he felt was a stabbing pain at the small of his back. His eyes would not focus. Everything was dark—dark and blurred. He sensed he was on the ground, and dimly a flicker of conscious thought made him wonder if he'd been wounded.

Carefully he moved his hands. They worked. He tried sitting up. His back ached dully; then the sharper pain began. Half-sitting up, he felt a sick fear in the pit of his stomach. Resting on one palm, he reached for his back with the other, afraid of what he might find. The exertion brought more pain. But he felt no moisture, no ruptured flesh, no protruding bone. He looked back to discover that he'd been lying on a rugged rock.

Now, why would he go to sleep on a rock like that? Had he been drinking?

Remo sat up and looked around. There was something there. Even with his vision out of focus, he made out the front end of a bus. But there was something odd about it. It was too short. Remo looked further and not far away found another shape. His eyes started to clear and he realized that the second shape was a bus too.

But there was only one bus. It had been cut in half. He was looking at the rear half, open in front like an old loaf of bread and spilling the charred remains of its seats.

Remo understood what had happened. An artillery shell. Or maybe a mine. He could see no bodies. He hoped there were none. He was wondering who'd been on the bus, when he noticed his feet.

His feet were encased in shoes. Where the hell were his boots? he wondered. Experimentally Remo tried to bend his legs. They were stiff, but they moved. He removed one shoe. A loafer. Good leather, too. Maybe Italian. Remo couldn't remember ever owning shoes of this quality before. Maybe he'd bought them in Saigon. Foreign goods were cheap in Saigon. But Remo couldn't remember having bought them. That wasn't his chief worry, however. He could see that he was somewhere out in the bush. Where the hell were his boots? Without them, he'd have immersion foot in no time. Assuming this was the rainy season. Funny, he couldn't remember that either.

Remo put the shoe back on and took a minute to breathe deeply. Then he got to his feet. His joints ached. He tried walking in a circle. Nothing damaged, just aches. He flexed his arms, working his biceps to get the night chill out of his muscles.

It was then that he noticed that his arms were bare.

"What the hell is this?" he asked aloud.

He was wearing a T-shirt. It was black, like his pants.

He looked around for his Marine uniform. There was nothing in sight. He had no pack, no canteen, no boots. He was dressed for shooting pool back in Newark, not for Vietnam.

Stiffly, apprehensively, he stumbled toward the front half of the bus. He clambered in through its gaping rear, which was tilted like a ramp. He found a Russian Kalashnikov rifle on the buckled floor. He checked the bolt. It worked. There were no bodies in the seats. Remo wondered where the driver was. His head throbbed. His ears felt like they had on the day he first landed in Saigon. It had been his first airplane flight, and during the descent, his eardrums had built up pressure until they ached. He hated the feeling and it hadn't gone away until he'd stepped off the plane with the rest of his company and the first trucks containing the aluminum coffins of dead American servicemen arrived to be loaded for the return flight. The shock had cleared his ears.

Remo felt like that now. He worked his jaw to clear his ears, but they remained stuffy, like blocked nasal passages.

Someone groaned. Remo ran to the other half of the bus. He pointed his rifle into the dark, tangled interior. Little steely glints like feral eyes winked back at him.

"Who's there?" he challenged. Another groan.

With his rifle barrel Remo knocked aside still-smoking seat covers. He stepped in gingerly, not trusting his light shoes. Again he felt the lack of boots as a dull fear in his gut. A man without boots in the jungle might as well shoot himself in the head and save himself a lot of unnecessary trouble.

Remo found a young girl, her face in shadow. She wore the black pajama uniform of the Vietnamese farmer—or the Vietcong. Probably a prisoner being transported, he decided.

Remo nudged her with the stock of his rifle. Her eyes snapped open and Remo was shocked by their color. They were *green*.

Ever since she was a child, Thao Ha Lan had had one dream. That the Americans would come back to Vietnam and crush the Hanoi regime. At night she dreamed that it would begin with the clatter of their helicopter gunships coming in low over the South China Sea. They would take Ho Chi Minh City first. And one special helicopter would come for her. Her father would be the pilot. Lan didn't know if her father had flown helicopters during the war. She only knew that her father was an American soldier. And American soldiers could do anything.

It was a dream her mother had impressed upon her. Her mother had loved an American serviceman. The American had died, her mother said. Lan did not believe her. She knew he lived in America, where there was no war, no fighting, no Communists. She hoped to go there one day. The dream survived the day her mother was taken away to a reeducation camp and even after she herself was taken off the Ho Chi Minh City streets.

The dream had flared anew at the arrival of the lone American with the dead, flat eyes that held no fear. The man had American features. Like her own. The only

American features Lan had ever seen belonged to the other *bui doi* who shared her work barracks.

It had been a crushing disappointment for Lan when the American had ordered them off the bus in the middle of the Cambodian jungle. She could not believe it. So when the American had finished putting gasoline in the bus, she slipped back aboard and hid in the darkened interior where she wouldn't be seen.

Lan was determined to go with the fearless American wherever he went.

Lan woke suddenly. She remembered the red flash. She felt herself tangled among broken bus seats. Then she saw the American. He was pointing a rifle at her face. He looked angry.

"Don't shoot. It Lan. Lan."

"Don't move," the American said. His voice was cold. Lan knew he was angry. She had expected that.

"I no move," Lan said. She folded her hands together to show they were empty. "I no move. Okay?"

"Where is this place?"

"Kampuchea."

"Never heard of it. You VC?"

"No. Not VC. VC all gone."

"Bull. Get up. Slow."

Still holding her hands together, Lan struggled into a kneeling position and bowed once to the American. She hoped Americans understood bowing.

"Skip that crap," the American told her. "On your feet."

Lan pushed herself to her feet. She took care to stand with her head bowed. She hoped the American would not send her away alone.

"Now, answer my questions, *bien*?" he said curtly. "Who was on that bus?"

Lan hesitated. She did not understand. The American glared at her. "Lan on bus," she said at last.

"Who else?"

"You. No one else."

"Who was driving? And don't tell me it was you."

"You drive. You drive to find American friend. Prisoner."

The American frowned. "This better not be a trick," he said. "Come on."

He stepped back to let her slide out of the ruined bus, and Lan stepped carefully to the ground. The American kept his weapon trained on her. He looked nervous and unsteady, not confident as he had before.

The American marched her around the shattered bus halves. In the middle of the road they found a sloping depression edged with splashed dirt.

"An antipersonnel mine," the American said, kicking at the dirt. His foot unearthed glinting steel balls. "It tore the bus in two. These are what were staring at me. I thought they were eyes."

Lan nodded. "Khmer Rouge mine."

"Khmer Rouge," the American said excitedly. "You mean Cambodians? Are we in Cambodia?"

"You not remember? You drive us here."

"Us? Us who?"

"Vietnamese prisoners. You free us."

The American looked at her confusedly. He shook his head, his dark eyes distracted.

"Where's the nearest American base camp? Tell me."

"Americans all gone. Long gone. None left."

"Then the next nearest camp. I've got to get back to my unit."

"Lan not understand. Not know where your American friends are. You search."

"I'll settled for an ARVN unit, then."

Lan grew frightened. This man was asking about the long-defeated Army of the Republic of Vietnam. Was he crazy?

"ARVN? No more ARVN. No more ARVN."

"What do you mean—no more ARVN?"

"ARVN surrender."

"Bull."

"Americans gone home. ARVN gone. No more South. No more North. War over."

"Over?" The American's voice growled. "Who won?"

"Communists. You not remember?"

"My ass. You're VC."

"You no understand. VC no more. ARVN crushed. Americans gone. War over. How I make you understand?"

"You can't, so forget it."

As Lan watched, the American started walking in circles. He put one hand to his head, never letting his eyes stray from her. Lan wondered if he was sick. She had never met any Americans before today. Did they always act so crazy when they were displeased?

"My head is killing me," the American moaned.

Then he dropped his rifle in the dirt and fell on it. He did not move after that.

13

Captain Dai Chim Sao returned to Hanoi via Moscow. He had slipped across the Mexican border and obtained an Aeroflot flight to the Soviet capital. It was a longer journey than going through Europe, but traveling by Western carrier would have placed him at the risk of arrest and extradition. Only Aeroflot was safe.

In Hanoi he was debriefed by Vietnam's defense minister.

"My mission was successful," Dai concluded after he'd finished his explanation. He stood at attention. The defense minister sat stolidly in his straight-backed chair. His office was decorated with standard Soviet-bloc orthodoxy. No shred of color or humor intruded upon its dark-wooded solidity. Dai waited for the at-ease order. It never came.

"Success is relative," the defense minister told him bluntly, and Captain Dai felt his heart sink. What had he done wrong? He cleared his throat prior to asking, but quickly realized that asking would be the same as accepting failure. Captain Dai was not ready to accept any such thing.

"The traitor Phong is dead," Dai repeated thickly. "My internationalist duty has been discharged."

"Had that man not escaped, you would not have had to risk the things you did risk."

"I am prepared to offer my life in service to the glorious revolution."

The defense minister waved his hand dismissively as if the life of one such as Captain Dai was something spent without thinking, like the number of dong required to purchase a cigarette.

"The American press are full of stories," the defense minister said. "The MIA issue, the POW issue. The killing of this Phong was broadcast live. The American government is upset. We were approaching an understanding, but now the political pressure on them to withhold diplomatic recognition until this is settled is enormous. Long months of quiet diplomacy have been jeopardized."

"I did what I had to do."

"In full view of television cameras," said the defense minister bitterly. He shook his iron-gray head.

"It was either there or not at all. Phong was guarded like a diplomat. It was only my resourcefulness that enabled me to gain admittance to the audience."

"You sound like the train engineer who left the brakes off and then congratulated himself for his heroism in stopping the runaway locomotive. Do not congratulate yourself while in this office, Comrade Captain. Your best does not impress me."

Captain Dai said nothing. His mouth ached for a cigarette, but he dared not light up while standing at attention.

The silence in the room lengthened. Finally the defense minister said, "We may have to kill the American prisoners."

"I will gladly undertake that task, Comrade Defense Minister."

"I am sure that you would. Your bloodthirsty kind enabled us to defeat the Americans. But you are now a liability. Why do you think you have been stuck in a distant camp post?"

"I considered it my duty," Dai croaked. His face was gray.

"And if I say it is your duty, you will kill the Americans with your bare hands. But that decision has not been made. For you, there is another duty."

"I stand ready."

"An American has broken away from a tour group near Ho Chi Minh City. No doubt it is the fault of the soft people of the South, who will never be purged of their capitalistic ways."

"We in the North are strong."

"We in the North are in charge," snapped the defense minister. "This American attacked a reeducation camp. He escaped with perhaps twenty *bui doi*."

Captain Dai would have spat on the floor in contempt, but spitting in public was forbidden in the united Vietnam.

"This American was last seen driving to the Kampuchean border. Before he ran amok he is reported to have made provocative statements about American POW's. We believe he may be an American intelligence agent sent here to conduct reconnaissance probes. If so, he is very clumsy in his work. But he is a skillful soldier. We cannot find him. That will be your job."

"I will return to this office and report unqualified success."

"I do not care if I ever see you again, Comrade Captain," the defense minister said with open contempt. "I hope the American shoots you dead at the same moment you obliterate him. Then two thorns in my side will be removed with one stroke."

"I will redeem myself."

"Not in these eyes. Dismissed."

Swallowing the bitterness that promised to creep into his voice, Captain Dai saluted smartly and turned on his heel. He was near tears. He had always considered himself a war hero. Now he knew that he had been just a tool. One mistake and they were ready to throw him away. He was certain that even the defeated Americans treated their war heroes better than he had been.

At first light Remo awoke. He was aware of the heavy smell of wet jungle, that unbelievably fecund smell that excited the nostrils. His eyes came open slowly, the hammering of a heavy rain on metal registering on his dazed brain before the light hit his retina.

Remo saw that he was inside the front part of the destroyed bus. A lashing rain made it impossible to see out the windows. He was lying on a pile of seat cushions, his rifle beside him.

The Vietnamese girl who called herself Lan slept nearby.

Remo looked around. They were alone. Out through the gaping, open end of the bus, he could see rainwater pelting twin shallow grooves obviously made when he'd been dragged into the bus. He looked at his heels. They were dirty, caked with red earth.

The girl. Obviously. She had dragged him here after he collapsed. Why had she done that? Remo picked up his rifle and checked it. The magazine was half-full.

Remo climbed over a tangle of seats and shook the girl awake.

She roused slowly. At the sight of his face, she smiled tentatively and Remo wondered if he'd been wrong about her. A VC agent would have shot him without mercy.

"You are awake," she said simply.

"Yeah." He didn't know what else to say. He looked at her face carefully. Her features were not like those of any Vietnamese he had ever seen. Those green, almond-shaped eyes. And those spots on her cheeks. He'd thought they were some kind of tropical skin disease, but they were freckles. Freckles!

"Lan help you. Lan your friend. You remember now?"

"No. I don't remember you."

Lan's smile faded like a cloud intercepting sunlight.

"Oh. Lan sorry."

"You know, I think you are."

"Am."

"I don't know too many Vietnamese."

"That okay. I not know any American before you."

The rain stopped. It was like a faucet shutting off.

"We can't stay here," Remo said. "You say we're in Cambodia?"

"Called Kampuchea now."

Remo made a face. "Yeah, right. Look, do you know which direction Saigon is?"

Lan stared at him uncomprehendingly.

"*Toi Muon di Saigon*," Remo said in Vietnamese.

Lan shook her head. "Not called Saigon anymore. Ho Chi Minh City."

"Are we going to have to go through that again?"

"Telling truth," Lan said testily. "Saigon old name. New name Ho Chi Minh City."

Remo sighed. "How far?"

"One night's drive. That way."

"Maybe we can reach the command headquarters in An Loc."

"An Loc dangerous. Much fighting."

"I thought you said the war was over."

"For Vietnamese, war never end. Vietnamese Communists fight Khmer Rouge Communists now."

"There's a switch," Remo said. He slid down out of the shattered bus and swore when his feet touched the muddy ground. He had forgotten that he had no boots. His shoes sank, cold, wet mud moistening the socks at his ankles.

"Damn. I could lose my feet walking around like this."

"We must go. Very dangerous here too."

"Then we walk. You say your name is Lan?"

"Yes, Lan. And you?"

"What about me?"

"Not know your own name?"

"Of course I do. I thought you said you knew me. I wish you'd get your story straight."

"Do know you," Lan said firmly. "You rescue me from camp. Not know your name."

"Remo. U.S. Marines."

"Ah," Lan said. "Marines number one!"

Remo laughed. "Yeah. We're number one, all right. Come on."

They followed the dirt road until it spilled into a blacktop highway. Remo took off his shoes and socks and carried them. The morning sun would dry them off quickly. For now, he was better off walking barefoot. The heat of the day warmed the road. Rainwater steamed off it like water on a skillet.

They walked for miles, encountering no traffic. Then, out of the north came a familiar sound.

"Helicopter," Remo said.

Lan grabbed his belt and tried to pull him off the road.

"Hey! Cut it out," Remo snapped, breaking free. Lan grabbed his wrists this time and strained against him.

"Out of sight," she begged. "Hide. Helicopter come."

"That's the idea. They'll pick us up."

"No. Not American helicopter. Vietnamese."

"Crap. The Vietnamese don't have helicopters. Sounds like an American Huey."

The rotor noise grew louder. Lan pulled harder.

"Look," Remo yelled. "Don't make me get rough. Run if you want. I'm staying in the open."

Remo stripped off his T-shirt and faced the direction of the approaching helicopter clatter. Lan broke for the roadside trees and hunkered down fearfully.

The helicopter lifted into sight up ahead. It was a wide-bodied craft with stub wings heavy with rockets.

It seemed to be following the road carefully, as if searching.

"Great," Remo muttered. "They can't miss me."

He started waving his shirt.

"Hey! American on the ground," he shouted. "I need a dustoff."

The helicopter skimmed over Remo as if it hadn't noticed him. Remo jumped around to face it, still waving his shirt and shouting.

"Hey, come back."

The helicopter did just that. It flashed around in a tight circle. And as it turned, Remo saw the yellow star in a red field that told him he was trying to flag down the wrong side.

"Oh, shit," he said. "The Vietnamese have helicopters now."

"I tell you!" Lan called. "Now you hurry."

Remo dived off the road. He took a position between two tall trees, well away from Lan. He brought his rifle up. He waited.

The helicopter hovered ominously above, searching.

Remo held his fire. The helicopter began to settle and he knew they'd spotted him.

Then Lan dashed across the highway under the gunship and to the other side of the road. She shouted at the top of her voice.

The helicopter suddenly rose in the air and peeled off after her. A chin-mounted Gatling gun opened up. It blasted the rubber trees until they stood like broken milkweeds.

"Dammit!" Remo shouted. He came out of cover and emptied his rifle after the helicopter, firing single shots.

The big tail rotor suddenly made a pinging sound and began wobbling wildly on its axis. A lucky shot had clipped it. The rotor stopped dead, and without its stabilizing influence, the helicopter began a slow pirouette in place, like a ridiculous Christmas-tree ornament spinning on a thread.

The helicopter pilot had no other option and he knew it. He let the chopper settle. It sank into the trees steadily until the main rotor encountered the treetops. Then all hell broke loose. Breaking branches flew like shrapnel. Someone screamed.

"Lan!" Remo yelled.

The helicopter suddenly stopped, its main rotor banged into a tangle of metal. The gunship hung in a net of foliage several feet off the ground. Men started jumping out of the open doors.

Remo saw that they carried rifles. He ran toward them. Unless he hit them first, while they were shaken up, the advantage would be theirs.

Dashing across the road, he plunged into the bush. He moved in a low crouch, the AK-47 feeling strange in his hands. He was used to an M-16. The helicopter hung like an enormous rotting fruit among tangled trees. A Vietnamese soldier was clambering out of the gun door, his rifle slung over his shoulder. Remo lifted his own assault rifle and squeezed off a single shot.

The gun clicked. He tried again. Nothing. Remo dropped into the grass and pulled the clip. Empty. The Vietnamese soldier was hanging by both hands from the chopper skid. He dangled momentarily, then dropped to the ground.

Remo dropped his useless weapon and eased forward. The Vietnamese was standing with his back toward him, unlimbering his rifle from his shoulder. Remo made a fist and came up like a ghost rising from a grave. The Vietnamese picked that moment to turn around. He saw Remo's fist and screeched in fright.

It was too late for Remo to pull his punch. It flew past the soldier's shoulder. Remo felt his legs being kicked out from under him. The two men landed in a tangle, Remo on the bottom.

Furiously Remo tried to fend off the soldier's flailing blows, but his hands wouldn't do what he willed them to. Every time he made a fist, it felt wrong. He found himself warding off the blows with quick, openhanded thrusts. What the hell was happening to him?

Remo grabbed the man's wrists. The two of them struggled. Then the soldier collapsed on top of Remo. Remo shoved him off and found Lan standing beside him, the soldier's AK-47 in her hands. It was pointing at him. This is it, he thought. I'm dead. But, wild-eyed, Lan tossed the weapon to him.

Remo caught it and spun on the sounds of approaching soldiers. There were two of them. They yelled like Indians as they charged through the grass. Remo set the fire selector to automatic and pulled the trigger.

Nothing happened.

"Damn!" he said.

"What wrong? Why you not shoot?"

Remo looked at the breech. It was fouled with mud.

"Damn!" he said again. He threw the rifle away. "Run, Lan!"

"No!"

He gave her a cruel shove. *"Di-di mau!"*

Lan stumbled away. Remo cut off in a different direction. The soldiers would be after him first. He got behind a thick-boled tree. He forced his right hand into a fist and listened for the clump of boots.

He saw the sweeping muzzle of a rifle before he saw the soldier himself. Remo waited tensely. One step, then two. When the man's flat-nosed profile came in sight, only inches away from Remo's face, he uncorked a roundhouse swing.

Remo never felt his fist connect. Suddenly his face was wet with blood and bits of matter and he stumbled back, wondering if he had been shot or had stepped on a mine.

He wiped his face desperately. His hands were covered with blood. His first thought was: Oh, God, I'm wounded. Then he noticed the soldier.

He was lying on his back, his head turned completely around so that the back of his head was where his face should have been. His fingers and feet twitched in the nerve spasms of near-death.

Remo knelt down and pushed the man off his rifle. He checked the breech. It seemed unobstructed. Then Remo saw the man's face and backed away in horror.

The man's jaw was shoved up under his right ear. The jaw was shapeless, as if the bone had been pulverized. His neck was obviously broken too.

Remo checked himself for similar damage, but other than the blood on his fist and face, he was uninjured. Then he noticed a patch of human skin clinging to one knuckle and wondered how he had skinned his knuckles if he hadn't connected. He peeled off the patch and saw the skin underneath was undamaged. In spite of the danger all around him, he blurted out in English, "Did I do that?" He looked at his fist stupidly and wiped the blood off on his pants.

Crunching sounds told him the other Vietnamese was getting close. Remo ducked behind the tree.

"Let's see if this works a second time," he said under his breath. He made a fist. It felt strange to make a fist. As a kid growing up in Newark, making a fist was second nature. Not now. Weird.

This time Remo didn't wait for the soldier to come into view. He sensed when he was close and jumped into his face. Remo's punch connected before the other man could snap off a shot.

The impact sounded like a beanbag under a sledgehammer blow. Remo felt hard bone turn to grit under his knuckles. The soldier's arms flailed like he was trying to balance atop a high wire. When he went down, he lay still. His face was a smear of red, and

Remo, who had seen terrible things in Vietnam, turned away, heaving.

He found Lan crouching by the roadside.

"You okay?" he asked.

"Lan okay. And you?"

"I'm not sure," he admitted, breathing hard.

"Soldiers dead?"

"They won't be bothering us," Remo told her. He plucked thick rubber-tree leaves off with his hands. They were still wet from the night rain, and with several of them he got most of the blood off his hands.

When he was done, he turned to Lan. "Thanks," he said.

"For what?"

"For helping."

"You helped me before."

"I don't remember that. I told you."

Lan's eyebrows drew together quizzically. "What do you remember?"

Remo sat down with his back to the alligator-hide bark of a rubber tree and looked up into the too-bright morning sky.

"Vietnam," he said distantly. "I remember Vietnam."

14

The Hind gunship deposited Captain Dai Chim Sao at a staging area twelve miles inside the Cambodian border.

Dai stepped off the skid before it fully settled on the ground. The rotors kicked up the reddish-brown dust of the dry season. He pinched his eyes shut to keep out the grit.

A short, buck-toothed officer hurried up to greet him.

"Captain Dai?" he asked.

"Who else would I be? What can you tell me about the American?"

"We know he is in this sector," said the officer, leading Dai to a string of waiting T-72 tanks. "One of our patrol helicopters radioed that it had found him. Then all communication ceased. We think the helicopter has been lost."

"How far?"

"Ten kilometers south. Not more than fifteen. Do you wish to lead the convoy?"

"That is my duty," said Captain Dai, climbing into the passenger seat of a Land Rover. He struck the driver on the shoulder as a sign to proceed. "I will not shirk it."

The officer jumped into the back as the Land Rover turned smartly and took the south road.

"You do not waste time," said the officer, waving for the tanks to fall in line behind them.

"I have no time to waste," Captain Dai said grimly. He unholstered a nine-millimeter Sig Sauer pistol and made a show of checking the action.

This is a man trying to prove himself, the officer thought. It would not be a good assignment, even though the American was alone.

The sun wallowed high in the shimmering sky. But even at midday, there was no traffic on the road. Occasionally they came to a crater where a mine had gone off, and around the crater the shattered remains of a truck. One mangled door bore the flag decal of Vietnam.

"Khmer Rouge," Lan explained. "They fight the Vietnamese same way the VC used to fight Americans."

"Turned the tables, huh?" Remo mused. He was still trying to fit the pieces together. There was no question that things had changed. He trusted Lan now, even if he couldn't believe her story. Not entirely. Not yet.

"You say the war is over," Remo said. They stuck to the side of the road, just in case they had to melt into the tree line. Remo had stripped one Vietnamese of his uniform and boots, donning them only after he removed all insignias. It made him feel like a soldier again, even though everything was two sizes too small.

"Yes. War over long time. For America. Not for Vietnam. Always new war for Vietnam. Vietnam fight China after Americans go. Now fight Kampucheans. Tomorrow, who know?"

"How long has it been over?" Remo asked. He searched his mind for a familiar memory. Yesterday was a blank. He could not even remember last month. His memory was clearer the further back he searched it, but recent events were vague. It was like looking down a tunnel. The walls were dark. But there was daylight at the end. What was it they used to say about the light at the end of the tunnel?

"War over ten-fifteen years now. Long time."

Remo whirled. "Fifteen years!"

Lan stopped dead in her tracks. Remo snapped his rifle up defensively.

"I tell truth. Americans go in 1973. Saigon fall 1975."

"Crap!"

"Not crap. True. Lan tell truth!"

"And I suppose I've been asleep in a rice paddy all that time." Remo sneered. "Like freaking Rip Van Winkle."

"Not understand."

"The last thing I can remember is fighting in Vietnam. In 1968. What have I been doing for twenty years?"

Lan shrugged. "How Lan know? It your life."

Remo looked at her without speaking. Her face was troubled and confused. He wanted to believe that she was his friend—he desperately needed one—but her story was ridiculous. It was impossible.

"I don't know what I'm going to do with you," he said slowly.

"Do nothing, then. I go." And Lan turned on her heel and walked in the opposite direction. Remo watched her go, half-wistful, and half-afraid that if he turned his back she would back-shoot him. Maybe she was VC after all. Maybe he was being set up for some elaborate brainwashing trick. He wondered if he'd been drugged. He still felt light-headed.

Lan's hair switched like an angry pony's tail as she walked off. She did not look back. Not even as she disappeared around a bend in the road.

Remo stood in the middle of the road, feeling foolish.

"Aw, hell," he said, and started after her. He walked at first, then started running. His feet felt like lead in the canvas Vietnamese boots. Funny they would feel like that. American boots were heavier. Canvas boots shouldn't feel like lead weights on his feet. He was a marine. Yet he felt like his whole body was screwed up.

Maybe he had been asleep for years. What else would explain it all?

Automatic-weapons fire chattered not far off. Remo dashed into the bush.

"*Dung lai! Dung lai!*" a man's voice cracked. He was calling for someone to halt.

"*Khoung!* Remo!" It was Lan's voice.

And then an AK-47 opened up.

Remo hurtled down the road like a linebacker. He plunged into the trees when he got to the bend and came out beside a low-slung tank. A Vietnamese soldier up in the turret hatch was sweeping the road with a pedestal-mounted .50-caliber gun.

Remo picked him off with one shot.

There was another tank behind the first, and a third idling at the rear. A Land Rover sat on a flat tire in the mud. Three soldiers crouched behind it, working their weapons.

Remo saw Lan dart between two trees. The crouching soldiers opened up on her with small arms.

"Hey!" Remo yelled, trying to think of the worst curse in the Vietnamese tongue. "*Do may! Do may!*"

The soldiers turned at the sound of his voice. Remo waved at them, then vaulted onto the first tank and disappeared into the open turret hatch.

Captain Dai Chim Sao heard the American voice accuse him of sleeping with his mother, and a chill swept through him. He spun on his heels, still crouching. "There!" he pointed. "The American."

But before they could open up, he disappeared into the lead tank, past a dead machine-gunner. Muffled shots came from the tank's interior. Then there was silence.

"You and you," Dai said. "Lay down covering fire on that girl. I will get the American's body."

"How do you know he is dead?" the officer asked.

"Because there are three brave Vietnamese soldiers in that tank. They have shot him. Do as I say."

The officer shrugged and started firing at the trees.

Captain Dai ran for the shelter of the far tank's tread, worked his way back, and climbed onto the rear deck.

Just as quickly, he jumped back onto the road.

The tapered turret was swinging around, its .125-millimeter smoothbore cannon nearly knocking him in the head. What was happening?

When the turret was pointing back at the other tanks, the cannon fired. Once, twice. Captain Dai screamed as the successive concussions pounded his eardrums. He hugged the ground. Shrapnel flew. A steel wheel wobbled past his head and clattered to the ground like a manhole cover.

Captain Dai looked up. The second tank was in ruins. Then he got a blast of exhaust as the tank containing the American started up. Dai scrambled out of the way of a rolling tread as the tank jockeyed around the destroyed machine and bore down on the third T-72.

The hatches on the third tank popped and the crew came out like ants from an anthole. They poured off the tank's plate sides just in time. Captain Dai was certain his painful scream was louder than the cannon roar. The third tank took a direct hit. It was enveloped in flames.

Then the first tank rolled across the flattened front end of the damaged tank and worked back toward the Land Rover. The driver and the officer showed stern stuff. They bounced bullets off the tank before they split in opposite directions. The tank climbed across the Land Rover, mashing it flat. A tire burst under the pressure of those remorseless treads.

The tank kept going. And out of the open driver's hatch, an American voice boomed.

"Lan! Hop aboard. I'm not sure I can stop this thing."

Even though Captain Dai knew that the Amerasian

girl was about to jump out of the bush, he made no
attempt to stop her when she did. He stood there, his
pistol hanging loose and impotent at his side, as the girl
disappeared into the open turret hatch and clanged it
shut.

The T-72 continued on. There was nothing Captain
Dai could do but inhale its foul exhaust and fight back
the racking sobs of failure.

"See if there's any food in here," Remo said, straining in the driver's bucket to see through the periscope.
The seat was mounted low to accommodate someone of
Asian stature. Remo felt cramped in the tiny cockpit,
which was set in the tank body just in front on the
turret.

Lan stuck her head forward. "You believe Lan now?"

"I'm reserving judgment," Remo told her.

Lan shrugged. "Whatever that mean. I will look for
food." She stepped around the bodies of the tank crew
and opened steel ammunition boxes. They contained
ammo clips. There was a crate tucked under a shelf.
She lifted the lid.

"No food. But look."

Remo twisted around in his seat. He saw the gleaming stocks of new Kalashnikov assault rifles packed in
Cosmoline.

"Food would be better," he grunted.

Lan frowned.

Remo turned back to the periscope. Just in time. He
had steered the tank toward some trees. He corrected
the tank, his feet searching for the brake. He found it,
and the tank rumbled to a halt.

"I'd better get rid of these bodies," Remo said. "In
this heat they're going to stink."

"I help."

"You sit." Remo climbed back to the turret and hoisted
the bodies out the top hatch. He kicked them off the

back of the tank and climbed back in. He left the hatch open to ventilate the tank.

As he got the tank moving again, Remo motioned for Lan to sit behind him. She did so without speaking.

"You were pretty brave back there," he told her.

"Not brave. Scared."

"Same difference," Remo said, shooting her a smile. Lan bowed her head, but finally the smile was returned.

"We friends?"

"Yes," Lan said. "Friends." She shook his hand and Remo laughed at the gesture, although it touched him.

"A while back you said something about my American friends. What was that about?"

"You say you come to Vietnam to help other Americans. POW's."

"Prisoners? Of the Vietnamese?"

"Yes."

"Did I say where they were?"

"No. I think you not know."

"Great. I don't know where I am, where I've been, or where I should be going."

"Not my fault."

"I know. I wish my head would clear. I feel like I've got all the answers swimming around in my head, but the thoughts won't stop long enough for me to get a clear look at them."

"I know one thing."

"What's that?"

"We need food."

"Yeah, maybe we can find a friendly village."

"Not here. Not anywhere."

"We'll come up with something," Remo said. But he had no idea what.

They hadn't driven much further when the sunlight streaming through the open hatch was suddenly blocked. Remo looked up first. Then Lan screamed. Remo braked and wriggled back into the tank's main body.

A face was looking down at them. A thin face pocked like a golf course, with thin, cruel black eyes. There was something vaguely familiar about that face, Remo thought, but his eyes were focused on the pointing barrel of the pistol that was aimed at his face.

"*Dung lai!*" the Vietnamese screamed.

"Sure thing, buddy," Remo said, putting his hands up. "Just don't get excited." To Lan he whispered, "Stay calm. I can handle this jerk."

The Vietnamese screamed at them.

"What's he saying?" Remo asked Lan.

"He say get out of tank. Now."

"I'll go first," Remo said. He grabbed a pipelike handhold and climbed up. The Vietnamese—he was a captain, Remo realized—stepped back from the turret, and when Remo lifted his head out into the air, he suddenly felt his stomach go cold.

"No," he croaked. "Not you."

The Vietnamese screamed at him again.

"Yeah, sure, I'm coming," Remo said thickly as he got out of the tank. His legs felt rubbery. He held his hands at shoulder height, but they trembled.

"Captain Spook," Remo said dully. His eyes were sick.

Lan came out next.

The captain motioned for them to step to the rear of the tank.

"*Lai dai! Lai dai, maulen!*" he screamed. His face was a mask of pocked fury.

"*Cai gi?*" Remo asked. And received a slap in the face for his question. He had no idea what the man was screaming.

"He wants us to walk to back," Lan told him. "I think he plan kill us."

"Why not?" asked Remo, stepping toward the back. "He's dead. Why shouldn't we be too?"

"What you mean?"

"I know this guy. He's dead."

Lan said nothing.

When Remo reached the rear deck of the tank, the captain motioned for them to turn around. Remo did as he was told. Lan stood beside him. She trembled.

The cocking of the pistol told them they were going to be unceremoniously executed.

Remo started to react. But Lan was already in motion. She screamed. Not in fear, but in a high, keening rage. The Vietnamese captain, not expecting the sound, was paralyzed with shock.

Lan fell on him, yanking at his pistol. Remo swept in from the opposite side. He knocked the captain over with a body block. The captain rolled off the tank and scrambled for cover under the tank chassis.

Lan had his pistol. She was sweeping the sides of the tank with its muzzle. She fired once, hitting nothing.

Remo took the gun from her. "Forget it!"

"I will kill him!" Lan screamed.

"Not possible. You can't kill him. He's already dead!"

Lan looked at Remo doubtfully.

"Come on," Remo said, shoving her into the turret. He climbed down after her and pulled the hatch shut, heat or no heat. He felt an almost supernatural chill course through his body.

"Why you afraid?" Lan asked as Remo started the tank moving again. "Why you not stay and kill him?"

"It's a long story."

"We have long ride."

"I already killed that guy."

"When?"

Remo considered in silence. Finally he said, "Good question. I don't know. Seems like two, maybe three months ago. Maybe longer."

"He not dead now."

"No, he's not. But I killed him during the war. You *bien?*"

"No. Not understand."

"I killed him during the war. In 1967. And he pops up again, not only alive, but not any older. Certainly not fifteen or twenty years older."

"You not believe Lan again?"

"I don't know what to believe. I can't think of any sensible explanation."

"Maybe that man ghost?"

"He felt solid enough," Remo said, straining at the periscope. It showed unobstructed road ahead.

"Then maybe you are the ghost," Lan said.

And again Remo felt that supernatural chill ripple through his bones.

15

The Master of Sinanju had endured the indignity of the cramped cabin. He ignored the stale, tinny air and the offensive odors of meat that were inescapable in the bowels of the American submarine. The journey was long, arduous, and boring. But it was necessary if he was to be reunited with his son. Chiun was resolved to endure it all. Later he would visit his grievances upon Remo. Let Remo apologize for them.

But the Master of Sinanju would not endure the indignity of lack of respect.

"Look, grandpa," said the American sailor. "The water is only two feet deep on this bay. Just step off the raft and wade the rest of the way."

"I will not," Chiun snapped. "My kimono will be wetted."

"Hey, just lift your skirts," the sailor said.

"And expose my nakedness before the Vietnamese barbarians?"

"You're not Vietnamese?" a second sailor asked in surprise.

He was slapped for his impudence. The slap was hard.

"Oooww! What'd you do that for?"

"I will not be insulted by my inferiors."

"No offense. But when a U.S. submarine carries an Oriental all the way from Tokyo to Vietnam for a night dropoff, we kinda assume we're dropping off a Vietnamese."

"Vietnamese are inferior."

"To what?"

"To me."

The sailors exchanged uncomprehending shrugs.

"Our orders are not to touch sand," the first sailor said. "We brought you into shallow water. Now all you have to do is wade."

"No," said Chiun, standing up in the inflated raft. He folded his arms resolutely. He was determined.

"Hey, sit down. If we're seen, it could mean an international incident."

"I will accept an international incident," Chiun said firmly. "I will not wade in dirty Vietnamese water."

"Looks clean to me."

"It is dark. How can you tell it is not dirty?"

"How can you tell that it is?" the first sailor countered.

"It smells Vietnamese."

The two sailors looked at one another and shrugged again.

"How about we sneak in just a tad closer?" the first one asked the other.

Chiun's face relaxed slightly.

"But we can't touch sand," they repeated in one voice.

"Agreed," said the Master of Sinanju. And he stepped to the bow of the raft and tucked his long-nailed fingers into his kimono sleeves. The sea breeze toyed with his facial hair and his clear hazel eyes held a satisfied light.

The circumstances might not be ideal, but this was a historic moment. No Master of Sinanju had stepped on Vietnamese soil in many centuries. He wondered if there would be a welcoming committee. But then he realized with a droop of his lips that probably there would not be one. These Americans were so obsessed with secrecy, they probably hadn't informed the rulers in Hanoi that a Master of Sinanju was secretly being deposited upon their very shore.

When the raft was a yard from shore, the sailors dug in their paddles and stopped it dead.

"Think you can jump the last couple of feet?"

Chiun turned on them haughtily. "Jump?"

"Yeah, we can't touch sand. Orders."

"How about water?" asked Chiun, stubbing the raft with a toenail. The gray plastic burst. The raft began shipping water.

"Hey! What happened?" the second sailor demanded as water poured over his lap.

The Master of Sinanju stepped for shore and landed in a swirl of kimono skirts. He faced the disconcerted sailors, who were so afraid of being seen they sat hip-deep in Vietnamese water, their raft a flat plastic rug under them. He beamed.

"Do not worry," he told them. "So long as you remain seated thus, you will not touch sand and your superiors will not be displeased."

"Too late for that now. We gotta drag this thing onshore to patch it up."

"Inform your captain that I will signal him when I am ready to depart these shores," said Chiun, walking away.

"When will that be?" the first sailor asked as he got to his feet, dripping.

"Why, when I am finished, of course."

Although no Master of Sinanju had trafficked with the Vietnamese in centuries, Chiun was welcomed in the first village he happened upon.

The welcome was abject. Chiun had to dismember only two political officers in front of the simple peasants before they fell on their knees and bumped their heads in the dirt in the traditional full bow reserved for emperors and other high dignitaries.

The village elder, who was nearly Chiun's age, invited the Master of Sinanju to sup with them. And Chiun accepted a bowl of boiled rice laced with fish heads. He smiled in gratitude, but when no one was looking, he plucked the fish heads out and placed them under a stone. Only the Vietnamese would eat the worst part of the fish. Probably swallowed the eyes too.

When the simple meal was concluded, Chiun explained why he was here.

"I seek a white man. His name is unimportant, for what matter the names of whites?"

And the village elder's eyes crinkled in agreement. He, too, had no use for whites, and said so.

Having come to an understanding, Chiun asked if there was gossip of a white American having returned to Vietnam.

The village elder pretended to ponder Chiun's request, and made a show of searching his memory. But Chiun could tell by the gleam in his eyes that he had the answer at once. But the night was young and why speed through gossip when, with some thoughtful pauses, socializing could be stretched far, and more rice wine could be consumed?

Chiun waved the proffered cup of rice wine aside, pretending that he was not thirsty.

At length the elder, whose name was Ngo, spoke.

"There are stories of a white American causing havoc along the Kampuchean border. No one can catch this American. They seek and seek him. But he is not to be found. No one knows his purpose here. Some say openly that it is a prelude to the return of the American military."

"You believe this?"

"No. The Americans are long gone. Although I would not be displeased at their return. Things are not good under the Communists."

"European ideas are always backward," said Chiun.

And Ngo nodded sagely. It was good when two wise men came together like this, he thought, even though one of them was a mere Korean.

After more talk, Chiun declined the further hospitality of the village. He left Ngo at the edge of the village, saying, "I hope you will not be troubled by the dismembering of the soldiers of your village."

"They sneak food and try to take advantage of the women. They will not be missed by us, and tomorrow there will be two more just like them, wearing the same clothes and spouting the same revolutionary nonsense."

"Perhaps when the Communists die off, three or four centuries hence," said Chiun, "one of your descendants may call upon one of mine for service. The era of the Ammamese kings ended young and with its true glory unfulfilled."

"I will pass your wish along to my grandson, and he to his," promised Ngo.

And Chiun took his leave of the village, content that he had planted the seeds for future employment in a market long disowned by his recent ancestors. Perhaps, he thought, some good might come of Remo's disobedience after all.

16

Night fell with the guillotine suddenness of Vietnam.

Remo had left the main road. He jockeyed the tank over a low hill and onto a cratered road going north. From what Lan had told him, they were working up the Vietnamese-Cambodian border. Remo still had no idea where he was or what he should be doing. They had found a manioc field at midday, and cooked the sweet-potato-like vegetables in a Vietnamese pith helmet, but even a full stomach hadn't cleared Remo's mind.

The area was alive with patrols. But most of them ignored the tank, thinking it occupied by Vietnamese. Once, they were sniped at by peasants in black pajamas, who had only pistols and bolt-action rifles. They looked like VC, but Lan had explained that they were Cambodian peasants who fought the Vietnamese.

The whole world had been turned upside down. And Remo didn't know where in it he belonged anymore.

Lan was driving the tank. Remo was nerve-tired, and took the time to show her how to operate the clanking machine. He curled up in the back and tried to sleep.

Lan's whispered call snapped him awake.

"What?" Remo mumbled. His head felt drowsy.

"Strange man in middle of road. What I do?"

"Soldier?"

"No. Old man."

"Go around him."

"Cannot. Him block whole road."

"The entire road?" Remo repeated incredulously. "Who is he—old King Kong?"

"I try to turn. He step in way. I go other way. He always there."

"I'll scare him off," said Remo, grabbing his AK-47 and climbing up the turret. He popped the hatch and poked his head out.

The tank clattered to a halt.

The man couldn't have been much more than five feet tall. He was old, with a shiny head decorated with little puffs of hair over each ear. He wore a gaudy skirted outfit that Remo had never seen on a Vietnamese before.

Lan poked her head up beside Remo's.

"Is he a priest or something?" Remo asked quietly.

"Not know. Never see one like him."

"Tell him to get out of the way."

"Step aside, old man," Lan called in Vietnamese.

The old Oriental rattled back words in sharp Vietnamese.

"What'd he say?" Remo asked.

"He want to know if we've seen an American."

Remo pulled his helmet lower over his head.

"Ask him why."

"Why you seek an American?" Lan asked.

The old man squeaked back and Lan translated.

"He say that his business, not ours."

"Tell him to get out of the way, or be run over," Remo said, disappearing below. He got behind the handlebarlike lateral controls and started the tank up. He inched it forward.

The old man stepped toward him. Remo shifted the tank right. The old Oriental shifted in tandem.

"What's his problem?" Remo muttered.

Lan called down, "He says he wants a ride. He's tired of walking."

"Tell him to screw off."

"Tell him to what?"

"Never mind," Remo sighed, grabbing up his rifle. "There's only one way to convince him we mean business."

Remo popped the driver's hatch and stepped to the front of the tank. The old Oriental stood, arms tucked in voluminous sleeves, directly in front and beneath him.

Remo pointed the rifle at his stern, wrinkled face.

"Get lost," he said.

The Oriental's face suddenly lost its impassive demeanor.

"You," he shouted in squeaky, angry English. "Liar! Deceiver! You would do this to your own father? How could you leave me after I gave my word to your emperor?"

Surprised, Remo lowered his rifle.

"Who's he talking to, you or me?" he asked Lan.

"Not know."

"I think it's you. He says he's your father. "

"I would not have that . . . that white Vietnamese for an offspring," the old Oriental snapped. "You are quite bad enough. Have you taken leave of your senses? Look at you. That weapon. And a uniform? Really!"

"I think he talk to you," Lan said. "He look at you."

"You know me?" Remo asked.

"Has grief aged me so much that you do not recognize your own father, Remo?"

"Hey! How do you know my name?"

"Smith is greatly displeased. He has sent me to punish you for your vileness."

Remo snapped the AK-47 level.

"I don't know any Smith. And whatever gook trick you're trying to pull, pal, it won't work. Now get out of the way."

"You will need more than that clumsy boom stick to protect you from my wrath, insolent one." And the old man lunged at Remo.

Remo tried to duck out of the way. He didn't want to shoot the crazy old man. But he quickly regretted his hesitation.

The rifle was snapped from his hands and sent flying.

Remo put up his fists. A steel-hard finger stabbed him in the stomach and he doubled over and rolled off the tank.

The pain was worse than anything he had ever felt. Remo was certain the old gook had slipped a knife into his gut. It hurt like hell.

The Master of Sinanju watched his pupil writhe on the ground. Remo did not curse him or complain as he usually did. In truth, he looked in fear of his life. Chiun frowned.

Then Remo, trying to crawl away, encountered his rifle. He snapped it around and pointed it at Chiun. And in Remo's eyes there was hatred mixed with fear. He fired.

Chiun sidestepped the first bullet.

"Remo!"

"Die!" Remo said, firing again. This time he was on automatic and the Master of Sinanju had to leap up and over him. He landed behind Remo.

Remo was looking around frantically.

"Lan!" Remo cried desperately. "Where'd he go?"

"Behind you," the girl cried, pointing.

Remo spun around. He opened up again, and then the Master of Sinanju realized what it must be. Of course. It was Remo's turn. Very well, he thought to himself, two may play games.

The Master of Sinanju moved like an eel, flashing to the right of the bullet track and then cutting across it so swiftly that he passed between two bullets. It was too easy. The rifle was filled with tracer bullets, making the bullet stream look like green fireflies spitting toward him.

The rifle ran empty.

"Shit!" Remo swore.

"Are you quite through?" Chiun demanded, walking up to Remo. Remo fought to get to his feet. He clutched his stomach with one hand and tried to swipe at Chiun with the other. He grabbed the rifle by the stock. The blow was weak, the form ridiculous. Chiun snatched the rifle.

"Now it is my turn," he told Remo. He called up to Lan, "You, girl. I will need more bullets. Throw them to me."

"Are you crazy, you old buzzard?" Remo demanded. "She's with me."

"Buzzard!" Chiun's cheeks puffed out in rage. "How dare you speak to your father so?"

"Father! You are crazy. I never saw you before."

Chiun stopped. His beard trembled. His clear hazel eyes narrowed.

"You deny me?"

"Call it what you want."

"Never before has a pupil denied his Master."

"His what?"

It was then Chiun understood. It was instantly clear to him.

"I am Chiun, Master of Sinanju," he said formally.

"Never heard of you or it."

"And who is this girl?" Chiun asked.

"A friend of mine."

"Your taste in females is as desolate as ever."

"Up yours."

"I will ignore that," Chiun told him evenly.

"Ignore what you want, Uncle Ho. Just get out of the way. I have places to go."

"How can you go to those places if you do not know where they are?"

"What makes you say that?"

"Because if you knew where you were going, you would be there by now."

"What do you know about where I'm going?"

"I know because I know where you have been."

Remo climbed back into the tank. Lan came to help him when she saw he was having trouble moving. He was breathing raggedly.

"Do you not want your boom stick, O warrior?" Chiun asked him.

"Keep it, Ho. I have more just like it."

The Master of Sinanju took the rifle by muzzle and stock and brought his hands together. The rifle splintered its entire length. Even the metal splintered.

Remo turned at the shrill, tormented sound. His eyes widened at the sight of the old Oriental wiping his hands clean. The ruins of the Kalashnikov settled at his feet, barely recognizable.

"How'd you do that?"

"With ease," said Chiun, beaming. "It is called Sinanju."

"Is it like karate?" Remo asked.

"It is far superior. With Sinanju, I could reduce your tank machine to powder."

"No shit," Remo said skeptically.

"Indeed," Chiun replied haughtily. "I could teach you, perhaps?"

"Don't need it," Remo said, letting Lan help him into the driver's bucket. "I've got a right hook that can fell a tree." Why did he keep talking to the crazy old man?

"I could use a ride, for I am old and my feet tired."

"I'm sure there'll be a bus later on," Remo said. He reached up to pull the hatch closed after him. Something made him hesitate. He looked at the old Oriental who looked like Ho Chi Minh in drag. He didn't look familiar. But something kept him talking, something instinctive and familiar.

"You are cruel. I was wrong about you. You are not my son. My son would not leave me alone in the jungle to be eaten by tigers."

"I'm glad we have that settled," Remo said, clanging the hatch shut. He had gotten the last word. Somehow that made him feel good. But when he painfully inserted himself in the driver's seat and started the tank, he felt a vague, elusive sadness—as if he were leaving something behind. Something important.

The Master of Sinanju watched the tank containing his pupil chug off into the night. He knew that Remo was not driving off in a huff. This was for real. He hadn't defended himself from Chiun's spiteful but harmless blow. His hands reeked of burned gunpowder and he was consorting with a Vietnamese.

Smith had been correct. Remo had backflashed. He had backflashed so far he no longer remembered the Master of Sinanju.

And worse, he no longer remembered Sinanju.

The Master of Sinanju sniffed the air. There were other ways to journey through Cambodia. Many other ways. He set off into the jungle to find one of them. The Master of Sinanju knew where Remo was going even if Remo himself did not. When Remo reached his destination, the Master of Sinanju would be waiting for him there.

17

Captain Dai Chim Sao did not admit defeat. He would not admit defeat. He could not admit defeat.

Returning to the base camp on foot, he informed the second in command, Captain Tin, that he had located the renegade American.

"My forces have him surrounded," Dai said rapidly. "It is just a matter of time now." He did not tell about the destroyed tanks. Or the soldiers who deserted under fire. Or how he had lain in the middle of the road for more than an hour, curled in a fetal position, after the tank had rolled over him. None of it.

"It will be dark soon," said Tin. "Do you need more men?"

"I need all of your men. Assemble them at once," Captain Dai ordered him stiffly.

"But if you have the American surrounded, then—"

"He could escape our cordon under cover of darkness," Dai snapped. "I will not take that chance."

"But if we deploy our entire force, who will defend this camp?"

"You will," said Captain Dai. "You will."

Captain Tin gulped and saluted. "Yes, Comrade Captain."

The Hind gunships lifted off first. Captain Dai was in the lead helicopter. The tanks followed with frustrating slowness. Captain Dai had a plan. He would lead the helicopters to the ruined tanks and express his surprise.

He would curse and rage and blame his men for having let the American turn the tide against them. His men could not contradict his story. Those who had not discredited themselves by desertion were dead. Then he would switch to the ground vehicles and lead the attack.

No one would know or believe that Captain Dai had led his unit into ignominious defeat. Especially after he snatched success from the dragon's jaws.

The jungle shivered under the rotors of the low-flying gunships. The whole night seemed to shiver. The sun took a long time to fall under the horizon. The night would come like a curtain closing on the final act of a play. Or on someone's life.

It would not close on his own, Captain Dai Chim Sao promised himself. On his sham career, perhaps, but not on his life.

Remo sat with his back to a tree. A leech dropped onto his hand and he quickly plucked it free before it could sink its teeth into him.

The moon was rising like a crystal globe. Remo watched its reflection in the still water of a rice paddy. Even in reflection, the moon looked too perfect, almost as if it had been sculptured of frosted glass. Remo stared at its icy surface, trying to see through it. He could not, of course. It only seemed transparent to the eye.

Lan slept nearby. They had pulled the tank into a thicket of bamboo. Wood smoke wafted from a nearby village. No one had come to bother them. Remo guessed they had wandered across the border into Vietnam. It was quieter. There were no sounds of distant conflict. It was like the Vietnam he always imagined would exist after the war.

According to Lan, it was. Remo looked at her face, composed in sleep. It was a trusting face. It was hard to believe such a face would concoct such a series of fabrications as she had tried to convince him were true.

But the other possibility was less plausible. The war was long over. America had withdrawn in defeat. Just that part alone was too much. And what was Remo doing in Vietnam twenty years after his last conscious memory of it?

On an impulse, Remo picked up his rifle, and walking low, worked his way toward the rice paddy. Its waters looked cool and inviting. But undrinkable without Halzatone tablets or boiling. He had no Halzatone, and lighting a fire was dangerous.

It was a perfect night for seeing. Not that Remo needed the moonlight. He had done so much night fighting during the war that he had taken to sleeping by day and avoiding artificial light. It built up his night vision until he could see like a cat.

That ability hadn't left him. It made Remo wonder. Where had he been all these years? Why couldn't he remember? As a kid he'd read stories about Japanese soldiers who were found hiding in the jungles of remote Pacific islands, unaware that World War II had ended long ago.

Was Remo like that? Had he been lost in the jungle, left behind? And what about his memory? He knew who he was, so he guessed that he wasn't suffering from amnesia.

The rice paddy was a perfect mirror. Remo crawled onto an earthen dike and looked down. His face was in shadow, his eyes hidden in hollows so that his face resembled a skull with flesh.

Leaning on his rifle, Remo got down on hands and knees for a closer look. He got a shock.

His face looked different, his eyes more deeply set than he remembered, the skin drawn tightly over high cheekbones. He didn't look nineteen anymore. But he didn't look twenty years older, either.

He was older—but not a lot older. It was his face, yes. But there were subtle differences. What did it mean?

When he got back to the tank, Remo sat down beside Lan. He stared at her innocent face as if something in her childlike features would reveal the truth.

Finally he shook her awake.

Lan rubbed her green eyes sleepily.

"My time to watch?" she asked, pushing herself up.

"Later," Remo said.

Lan saw the stern look in his face. "What?"

"I have to know the truth."

"What truth?"

"The truth about the war," Remo snapped, shaking her shoulders. Lan recoiled from his touch.

"You hurt me." She kneaded her shoulders where Remo's hard fingers had dug into the soft flesh.

"Sorry," Remo said in a quieter voice. "I just can't make sense of it."

Lan looked away. "Not my fault."

"The war is over?"

"Yes."

"You're sure of that?"

"Yes." Her eyes were sullen.

"I looked at myself in the rice paddy. I look older."

"Of course."

"But not that much older. Not twenty years older."

Lan said nothing.

"I can't have been wandering the jungle for twenty years without growing older or being captured."

"You show up at reeducation camp. Not know where you come from. You rescue Lan. Rescue Lan's friends too. Friends very grateful. You leave us, but Lan not want to leave you. Lan like you. Lan sneak back on bus. You drive away. Then bus hit mine. You wake up. Lan wake up. Rest you know. Lan stand guard now?"

"Later," Remo said. "Listen, I think I believe you. But there are things I can't explain. Except one way."

Lan tossed her long hair back. "Yes?"

"When the bus hit the mine, it was pretty torn up."

"Yes. Cut in two."

"Don't you think it's strange that we both survived? The thing was riddled with steel pellets."

Lan shrugged. "You in front. Lan hiding in back. Bus hit mine, break in middle. Not strange. Lucky."

"What if we only *think* we're alive?"

Lan looked at Remo uncomprehendingly.

"What if we're dead?" Remo said flatly.

"No!" Lan cried, scrambling to her feet. Her face shook with anger. "Lan not dead. No! You dead, maybe. Not Lan!" She backed away from Remo in fear.

"Look," Remo said, getting to his feet. "I don't want to believe it either. But it fits. It even explains Captain Spook. We're the walking wounded, dead but still fighting on."

"No, not fit."

"You said it first, remember? Maybe I'm a ghost. I can't remember anything but the war. I must have been killed driving that bus."

"No. Lan not killed in war. Lan born during war, grow up after. Mother teacher, taken away when Lan young. Lan live on street. Later, Lan taken to reeducation camp. Lan not die in war. Lan not die ever!"

Lan broke down sobbing. She fell to her knees and buried her face in the cool grass.

"Lan not die ever!" she repeated brokenly.

Remo knelt beside her. He brushed her long black hair away from her face.

"Maybe you're right," he said quietly. "I just can't figure it out."

"Remo think too much. Should be like Lan. Not think. Feel. Feel with heart."

"Yeah? What do you feel?"

Lan gathered her legs under her. She sat up. Her eyes were red around the edges.

"Lan feel sad. Feel ache. Lan think it love."

"Me?"

"Since Lan child, Lan's mother told her about American father. His name Bob. Bob come back someday, Lan's mother say. Come back and take us to America. But Bob not come. No American come. Then Lan's mother say Bob dead. Lan not believe. Bad things happen to Lan. Then you come. Lan like you because you American. Now Lan like you because you Remo."

"I like you too. But you're just a kid." Remo's face froze. "Funny."

"Lan not funny."

"No, I didn't mean it like that. The last I remember, I was nineteen. You look about that. But somehow I think of you as a kid. Like somewhere in my head I know I'm older."

"Not understand."

"Me neither. And what was that old Oriental's problem? He knew my name. He said he was my father. I never knew my father, but there's no way my father was Vietnamese—or whatever he was."

"He very strong," Lan said.

"Yeah, but so am I." He looked at his fist. "I killed two guys with single punches. I don't ever remember being that strong."

"Lan tired of thinking."

Remo grinned suddenly. "Me too."

Lan smiled shyly. She touched his arm tentatively.

"Remo like Lan?" she asked softly.

"Yeah, sure I do."

"Love Lan now?"

"What?"

"Love. Love Lan now?"

"I don't know. I'm just getting to know you. I do like you, though."

"Love Lan later, then. Make boom-boom now?"

"Oh," said Remo, suddenly understanding.

"Okay?"

Lan peeled off her shirt. Her skin was pale in the moonlight, her breasts small but firm. She put her arms around Remo's neck and pushed him to the ground gently. Her little mouth took his hungrily.

When they broke apart, Remo whispered, "That was pretty good." He took her by her tawny waist.

"Maybe if Remo make boom-boom, Remo understand he is alive, not dead, not ghost. Maybe we both feel alive."

"It's worth trying," Remo said, pushing her down into the cool grass.

In his perch in a nearby tree, the Master of Sinanju made a disgusted sound. He turned around and faced the east, where the sun would soon rise. Without knowledge of who he was, Remo had reverted to his most base nature.

When the sounds coming to his fragile ears told him that Remo was actually enjoying himself, and therefore not employing correct Sinanju love techniques, Chiun knew for certain that Remo had lost his knowledge of Sinanju. He was actually performing sex as a pleasure, not a duty. Chiun clapped his hands over his ears to block out the animal moans of backsliding.

18

Remo woke first. He woke instantly, some instinct pulling him from sleep. He raised himself up on one arm, listening.

Lan clung to him. He reached over and threw her shirt across her naked shoulders. Her mouth moved as if she were speaking to him. Remo bent an ear. Her words were vague mumbles, not English. Not even Vietnamese. But subvocal mutterings.

Remo decided that Lan wasn't making the sounds that woke him.

Then they came out of the north. First one. Then two more.

Helicopter gunships. They flashed overhead so fast there was almost no warning of their approach.

Remo shook Lan briskly. "Lan! Wake up."

"Remo?"

"Choppers. They probably spotted the tank. We gotta *di-di* out of here."

Lan quickly scooped up her clothes and followed Remo into the tank. They dressed frantically. Remo got the tank going. He sent it grumbling up onto the road.

The choppers came around on another searching pass.

On the third pass, one cut loose with a rocket. It struck fifty yards up the road. Dirt and rocks mushroomed. Dust billowed into the periscope. When it cleared. Remo saw a gaping crater.

"Those are antitank rockets," he yelled as he sent

the tank skittering around. "One direct hit and it's all over."

Lan grabbed up an AK-47 and popped the main hatch. She opened up into the sky. Her firing was wild and indiscriminate.

"Don't waste ammo," Remo yelled after her. He had the tank turned around. He hit the gas. Of course, it was hopeless. No way they could outrun three fast gunships.

"I keep them away," Lan called down between bursts.

"For how long? They're faster and more maneuverable."

"Have to try," Lan shouted down. Then she emptied another precious clip.

"Damn!" Remo said.

Then the gunships ripped across his line of sight again. One of them peeled off from the group and cut loose with another rocket. The *whoosh* sound made Remo's blood go cold.

Remo jumped up and pulled Lan down by the seat of her pants. They fell together in a tumble. Remo felt a bare breast under one hand. Lan hadn't had time to button her shirt. He pressed her to the floor, using his own body as a shield. No time to close the hatch. It wouldn't matter under a direct hit.

There was no direct hit. The concussion sound came from the front. Dust and grit rained down the turret hatch.

Remo got up. He scrawled forward into the cockpit. There he saw another crater ahead.

Lan joined him. "They miss again," she said.

"I think it was deliberate," Remo said. "They want to stop us here. Probably means reinforcements on the way."

"We dead?"

"Maybe not. They might want us alive."

"Better off dead," Lan said, buttoning her shirt.

"Look, you stay with the tank."

Lan's eyes widened. "You leave Lan?"

"They're probably sending more tanks. I took over one. I can take over others."

"Okay," Lan said. "Hurry back. Do not get killed."

"It's not in my plans," Remo said. And he kissed her.

Remo waited until the gunships dropped behind the trees before he slipped out the hatch. He jumped into the roadside bamboo. The sun was sending mists rising off the rice paddies. It was warming up. He found a sturdy tree and got into the high branches. He had a full clip in his rifle and three more in his pockets. He waited.

As Remo had guessed, the convoy came out of the north, as had the helicopters. There were three tanks, led by a Land Rover. Remo recognized the pockmarked face of the NVA officer he knew as Captain Spook in the back of the Land Rover.

Remo raised his rifle and got the man in his sights. But no, that would spoil the element of surprise. He lowered the rifle.

"You got more lives than a cat, pal. But today they run out. That's a promise."

Remo shouldered his rifle and crawled out on a limb as far as he could. He hung over the road. The tanks ran with their turrets open, soldiers manning swiveling .50-caliber machine guns. Remo waited until the first two tanks had passed. He dropped from his perch just as the third tank rolled under him.

Remo landed behind the turret. He landed clumsily. The boots. They felt wrong. He clung to a bulkhead to keep from falling off. When he regained his balance, he inched up toward the turret.

The machine-gunner never heard Remo's approach. Remo smashed him in the back of the head with a single blow. The soldier slumped over his weapon.

Remo lifted him out of the hatch bodily, surprised at

his own strength. He threw the man overboard and took his place.

Carefully, hoping the crew below wouldn't notice the substitution, Remo unlimbered his rifle. He set the selector to single shot. He waited.

Ahead, the Land Rover came to the first crater. It whirled around it. The first tank hadn't enough room. It clanked into the pit, treads digging into the broken asphalt for traction. The noise would cover the sound of single shots. Remo dropped into the tank and put his muzzle to the back of the driver's head.

The driver said nothing. He raised his hands.

The officer manning the cannon hadn't noticed Remo.

Covering the driver, Remo slipped up behind the weapons officer and slammed his face into the cannon breech with the butt of his rifle. Then he turned his attention back to the driver.

The driver's face was a mask of sweat.

"I don't want to kill you, pal," Remo told him, "although I'm not sure why I shouldn't."

"*Khoung! Khoung!*" the driver protested.

Remo knocked him over the head. He yanked him out of the bucket and got behind the lateral controls. Remo peered through the periscope. He had a clean shot at the tank up ahead. But even if he got it, the lead tank was in a position to return fire. The helicopters were still a factor too.

Remo decided to wait. The first tank clanked out of the road crater as the second flopped into it. Remo sent the tank inching ahead cautiously. He wasn't sure of his next move.

The helicopters decided him. One by one, they settled onto the road on the other side of Lan's tank, blocking it.

"Okay," Remo said. "Time to rock-and-roll."

Remo dug around in back. He found a crate of hand grenades and started stuffing them into his pockets. He came out through the driver's hatch and slipped to the ground.

Remo still wore the ill-fitting Vietnamese khaki and one of their avocado pith helmets. He walked casually up behind the other tanks, slouching to make himself appear shorter. He pulled the pin on a grenade and just as casually tossed it into the lap of the second tank's turret gunner.

The gunner screeched in fright and jumped off the turret. That was a big mistake. He should have tossed the grenade and jumped into the safety of the tank. Remo shot him. The grenade went off inside the tank.

The sound was muffled, but the smoke boiled out of every aperture like floating serpents.

Next, Remo jumped to the crater and tossed several grenades. He lay flat on the crater's lip. The concussions came like a string of exploding firecrackers, but much louder.

There were shouts from the lead and remaining tank.

Remo clambered into the crater, rushed past the fiery mess that was the second T-72, and lifted his head above the crater wall. The turret was slowly turning around. The machine-gunner was sweeping his perforated gun muzzle back and forth, his eyes staring stupidly under his pith helmet.

Remo took his head off with a short, concentrated burst and followed the bullets out of the crater. He was on the tank in an instant, pulling pins and popping grenades past the slumping, headless corpse.

The grenades went off. Brief flashes of fire spat from the ports. Remo was already into the roadside trees. He was taking fire from the Land Rover. The helicopters were powering up again.

"Lan!" Remo called. "Don't let them take off!"

Lan came up out of the turret and opened up. She had a rifle cradled under each arm. She braced herself against the hatch well and set the muzzles on the rim to steady them. She fired them alternately. Her body shook with the bone-rattling recoil.

Not designed for ground fighting, the gunships never had a chance. Their main rotors spun lazily, but the machines didn't lift off. The pilots were either wounded or running for their lives.

Meanwhile, Remo got behind some trees, working toward the Land Rover crew. He was back on single firing. He picked off the driver. Another soldier was flat on the ground, firing from under the chassis. Remo ducked behind sheltering trees, pulled a grenade pin, and rolled it along the road. It hit the left-front tire and rebounded onto the road.

The soldier under the vehicle saw the grenade lying mere inches in front of his face. He had no shelter, no time to wriggle out from under the vehicle—so he did the only thing left to him.

He struggled to reach the grenade with his hand. No doubt he hoped to lob it back at Remo. But there wasn't time. His shaking fingers touched the grenade, upsetting it. It popped out of reach. Then it exploded.

A piece of shrapnel embedded itself in a tree not far from Remo. It hit with a meaty thunk. Remo sat with his hands clamping his helmet down tightly.

When Remo looked out again, the Land Rover was burning. Something like a charred ham smoked under it.

But there was no sign of Captain Spook.

Remo looked frantically. There was no third body near the vehicle. Captain Spook had been in the Land Rover. Maybe he was in the trees on the other side of the road. But Remo saw nothing move.

"Lan! You see anyone else?"

Up in the turret, Lan swung around. Her face was a smear of dirt and sweat.

"No!" she shouted back.

"There's one running loose. Keep your eyes peeled."

"Keep what?"

"Just watch! We're not out of this yet."

Remo waited, crouching. Silence returned to the road. Insects resumed their multitudinous sounds. Nothing moved other than flame and the nervous twitching of the dead and dying.

Finally Remo decided to make for the tank. He retreated into the bush, worked forward, and flashed across the road.

Seeing him coming, Lan laid down covering fire. She shot at nothing and everything. She disappeared into the tank only after Remo dived into the driver's hatch.

Remo was breathing hard when he got behind the laterals.

"Button it up!" he panted. "We gotta get out of here. Fast!"

"Why?" Lan asked as she dogged her hatch shut. "You kill them all."

"Not him," said Remo. "Not Captain Spook. He vanished again."

"Who?"

"The NVA officer I killed. Back in the war. I saw him again. He's out there."

Remo sent the tank rumbling forward. It tipped as it slid down into the far, unobstructed crater.

"I think we can push those choppers aside and make a break for it," he observed.

"They will send more."

"Don't get discouraged," Remo said. "We've been doing pretty good so far." His breathing was more regular now. He wiped dirt off his forehead.

"Then why you look so scared?" Lan asked, jamming fresh clips into two rifles.

"I'm not afraid of anything."

"Not true. You fear Captain Spook. I see it on your face."

Remo said nothing. The crater filled his periscope.

He bounced in his seat, his shoulders striking the cramped cockpit walls. Lan hung to handholds. The tank ran level, then started to climb nose-first, its treads clawing out of the depression.

When the tank lumbered onto the road, Remo let out his breath.

"I thought we weren't going to make it for a minute," he said.

Then he added, "Oh, crap!"

"What?" Lan asked, leaning forward.

"Look."

Lan looked past Remo's shoulder. Through the narrow slit of the port she saw a man in a ragged Vietnamese officer's uniform standing in the center of the road. He carried a Kalashnikov rifle upended like a pole. A white rag fluttered from the muzzle.

Remo stopped the tank.

"He want to surrender," Lan said quietly.

"I don't trust him."

"Then run him over."

Remo considered. "Do no good," he said at last. "He's already dead. Grab your gun."

Remo pushed open his hatch. He pointed his weapon at Captain Spook's pock-marked face. Lan covered him with the turret gun.

Captain Dai Chim Sao shouted at him in Vietnamese.

"What's he saying?" Remo asked Lan.

"He say you destroy his unit."

"Tell him I noticed."

"He want to know what you want."

"I want to kill him for sure. No, don't say that."

"What I say to him?"

"Tell him," Remo said slowly, "tell him I want him to surrender."

Lan shouted Remo's answer in Vietnamese. Captain Dai yelled back.

"He say he already surrender," Lan explained.

"Not just him. Everybody. I want Vietnam to surrender. Unconditionally."

Lan told him. Captain Dai's mean face broke in shock. His answer was brittle.

"He say he only a captain. Cannot surrender whole government."

"Then tell him to kiss his butt good-bye," Remo hissed, lifting his rifle to shoulder-firing position.

Captain Dai dropped his rifle and shouted frantically.

"He say he can give you better than surrender," Lan said quickly.

"There's nothing better," Remo growled.

"He say he know where American POW's are held. He will take you. You take Americans away and leave Vietnam alone."

"That sounds like surrender to me," Remo said, lowering his rifle. "Tell him it's a deal."

19

Captain Dai Chim Sao knew he was finished. He had lost two entire tank groups to a lone American and a half-breed girl. Before his last soldier fell, Dai knew he would be disgraced. Death was not even a concern anymore.

And because he feared death less than disgrace, Captain Dai formulated a plan. He slipped away from the Land Rover as the last tank exploded in flames. He worked his way through the trees to the ruined helicopters and found a working radio.

He radioed his position and warned the surrounding base camps of his planned route.

"We are not to be intercepted," he had said. "That is an order. Obey me." And tying an oil rag to his rifle, he'd stepped into the path of the oncoming tank, knowing that at worst it would only crush him under its implacable treads.

But now Captain Dai was squatting under the muzzle of the smoothbore cannon, the *bui doi* girl holding him under the menace of the turret gun.

For hours, the tank rattled along the north road. It stopped only once to replenish its gas tank with fuel from the on-board supply.

The red sun beat down on Captain Dai's unprotected head. But his mean face was twisted in a wicked smile no one could see.

The American didn't know it, but he was riding into a trap.

*   *   *

Hours later, the tank was grumbling along a grass-choked jungle path. The path had obviously been knocked out of the jungle by many passing vehicles.

In the driver's bucket, Remo called up to Lan.

"Ask him how long till we reach the prison camp."

Lan spat out the question. She interpreted the captain's surly reply.

"He say soon, soon," Lan reported.

"He's said that before," Remo complained.

Lan said nothing. The path was narrowing. Remo had to expend most of his energy working the laterals to keep the treads from climbing the occasional too-close tree. It was work.

It was still light when Remo jockeyed the tank around a tight turn. The suddenness with which the jungle opened up around them took their breath away.

"Remo!" Lan called suddenly.

"Yeah, I see it," Remo said, craning to see through the periscope. "It's gotta be the camp."

"No," Lan said dully. "Not camp."

"Sure it is," Remo insisted.

"Yes, camp. But look to side."

Someone was shouting orders in brittle Vietnamese.

"Shut him up," Remo said, stopping the tank.

"Cannot," Lan said. "Not captain. Come up, Remo."

Remo climbed up to join Lan at the turret hatch. He looked around. Then he saw the other tank. It had been laying for them at the edge of the camp clearing. Like the finger of doom, its gleaming cannon was pointing directly at them.

Remo grabbed the turret gun. He pointed it at the back of Captain Dai's head.

"Tell them to back off or I'll blow his head open," Remo shouted.

Frightened, Lan relayed Remo's threat.

The tank commander stared back stonily. Remo

watched him out of the tail of his eye, afraid to tear his gaze from the back of Captain Dai's head. Dai turned. His face was alight. He bared his shovellike teeth in a sneering grin.

"Don't be so smug," Remo said. "I killed you once. I'll be happy to do it again."

Lan relayed Remo's words. Captain Dai's face lost its catlike grin. A variety of expressions crossed his features.

"What are they doing?" Remo whispered.

"Waiting," Lan said. Her face was drawn.

"For what?"

Then they knew. Out from behind the tank, a line of men marched with heads bowed and shoulders drooping. They wore gray cotton. They were Americans. Behind them marched others, who were not all American. Lan recognized them as her fellow Amerasians. Her throat tightened painfully at the realization that they hadn't made it to Thailand. To Remo, they meant nothing.

The stone-faced tank commander pointed to the line of captives. They were under the menace of several soldiers' rifles. The officer shouted angrily, gesticulating at Remo and again at the prisoners.

"Don't tell me," Remo told Lan. "We surrender or they get chopped down."

Lan nodded silently, fighting back tears.

Remo's fingers tightened on the machine-gun trip. He wanted very much to pull it. Captain Dai saw the look in Remo's eyes. His smile completely fled. Sweat broke out all over his unlovely face.

Finally Remo said, "You're not worth it," and backed away from the machine gun, its muzzle dropping impotently. Remo raised his hands.

"No choice, kid," he said thickly.

No longer fighting her tears, Lan threw her AK-47 into the dirt. She raised her hands.

"Good-bye, Remo," she whispered thickly.

"We're not dead yet."

The soldiers surrounded the tank and motioned Remo and Lan down from the turret. They forced them to kneel, their crude hands feeling their clothes for hidden weapons. Remo's helmet was cast aside. Others helped Captain Dai off the tank. He had difficulty walking. His knees wobbled.

Unsteadily he walked up to Remo and slapped his face twice, first in one direction and then with the back of his hand on the return sweep.

"*Hai cai nay ra!*" Dai screamed at the tank officer. Lan was dragged away to a thatched hut. The prisoners were marched after her.

Then they escorted Remo across the camp, taking him to the far side, where a bulky steel container about the size of a garbage dumpster stood in the dirt not far from—if the overpowering stench meant anything—an open latrine trench.

Remo was forced to kneel again, and the sudden night of Vietnam fell upon them. The refrigeratorlike door at one end of the long container was thrown open and Remo was kicked and jabbed into its dark interior.

The door clanged shut and the locking lever was thrown.

Remo found himself in a stifling cube of heat. The air was heavy with stale human smells. A little light filtered in through bullet holes in the sides.

Remo put an eye to one of the holes and tried to see outside. A low voice pulled him away from the hole.

"They don't usually put two men inside at once," it grumbled. "But I do appreciate the company."

"Who's there?" Remo asked.

"Who do you think, fool? Youngblood. You been brainwashed or something?"

"Youngblood?" Remo asked. "Dick?"

"Hey!" Youngblood suddenly shouted. "I don't recognize your voice. Who the hell are you?"

"It's me, Remo."

"Yeah? Remo who?"

"Williams. How many other Remos do you know?"

"Williams . . . Remo Williams. . . ." The voice was low, as if tasting the name. "I usta know a marine by that name."

"Dick. It's me."

"Prove it."

"Tell me how."

"Lemme see your face. Get over by the vent holes back here, where there's light."

Remo scrooched over. His eyes were becoming used to the lack of light. He made out a dim, hulking form with bright, suspicious eyes.

The eyes came closer. They were familiar. But not the surrounding face. It was thicker, the skin coarse and lined.

"Shee-it!" Youngblood said. "It is you, you sonovabitch!"

"You look old," Remo said slowly.

"The hell you say," Youngblood scoffed. "After twenty years, what did you expect, Nat King Fucking Cole?"

"Then it *is* true."

"What?"

"The war. It's over."

"You ain't heard?"

"I haven't been able to believe it," Remo admitted.

"Say! What the hell are you doin' here?"

"I don't know. I don't remember. I woke up and here I was."

"I enlisted, myself," Youngblood growled. "Thought you were drafted."

"They tell me it's been twenty years, but all I can remember is the war."

"They found you in the jungle, did they?"

"No, I captured a tank. I drove it here. They ambushed me. Another tank."

"An old T-54?"

"Yeah."

"Hah! You dumb shit. You got snookered. That thing's got a wooden cannon. It can't shoot riceballs."

"Well, you don't have to be so happy about it," Remo complained.

"Sorry, man. I been here so long I'll take my entertainment any flavor at all."

"Who else is here?"

"There's only seven of us now. There used to be more than thirty. I'm senior officer now. That's why they got me in this here conex. You'll love it. Like an oven during the day and an icebox at night. What happened was, a prisoner escaped. A Vietnamese named Phong. They got me in here as punishment. Hey, is that how you come to be here? Did Phong send you?"

"I told you, I can't remember what I'm doing here. In my head, it's still 1968."

Youngblood grunted a laugh. "Yeah, my watch kinda stopped too. You know, Remo, you look different."

"So?"

"I mean it. You look different. But not much older than I remember. Geez, wherever you been, man, you ain't aged a lick."

"I think I'm dead," Remo said hollowly.

"What?"

"I think I died in the bush. I'm a ghost."

"Hey now, man. Don't you be pulling any spook stuff on me. That shit don't go with me."

"Spook," Remo said. "That's the other thing. Remember Captain Spook? He's here. We killed him and he's still alive. What does that tell you?"

Dick Youngblood's low voice rose in gales of laughter. The conex shook with the enthusiasm of his howls.

"Remo, you are one confused fuck," he chortled. "But I know how you must be feeling. I felt my own ass pucker the first time he turned up in my face."

"Huh?"

"That ain't Captain Spook. That's Spook Junior. His son. Calls himself Captain Dai. They do seem to be painted with the same ugly stick, don't they?"

"Son?" Remo said in a dazed voice. Then, "Shh. I hear someone coming."

In the darkness, Dick Youngblood put an ear to the metal wall.

"I don't hear shit."

"Footsteps. Very quiet."

"You're hearing ghosts. Probably your relatives."

"Then I'm seeing them too," Remo said. "Look."

Youngblood let Remo guide him to a bullet hole.

"A gook," Youngblood said. "Old, too. Never seen him before."

"That's Uncle Ho."

"Ho Chi Minh is dead too, but if that's him, I take back everything I said."

"Uncle Ho is what I call him. I met him out in the bush."

"Just like that. Who is he?"

"I don't know his name. But he claims he's my father."

"Yeah, now that you mention it," Youngblood said dryly, "I can see the family resemblance."

The Master of Sinanju waited until the camp settled down for the night. He had patiently awaited the coming of his pupil to the Vietnamese prisoner camp. As always, Remo was late.

It had been simpler to allow Remo to be captured than to interfere. In Remo's present state, Chiun did not wish to risk losing him to wild gunfire. When he believed Remo had been in the big metal box long enough, Chiun approached silent and unseen by the few guards picketed about.

"Remo," he whispered.

"What do you want, Ho?" Remo asked in a surly tone.

"Simply to speak with you, my son," Chiun said
sweetly. "Are you comfortable?"

"Of course not. I'm a freaking prisoner."

"Oh," said the Master of Sinanju, as if just noticing
that fact. "Why do you not escape?"

"How?"

"These convenient holes," Chiun told him, inserting
a long-nailed finger into one of the bullet holes. "They
are just right. They make wonderful handholds with
which to tear off a nice section of wall."

"Watch it!" Remo barked. "You nearly poked my eye
out."

"Your fault for peeking. You do not need to see me to
understand my words."

"You're right, Remo," another voice said. "He is a
crazy old gook."

"Who is that?" demanded Chiun. "Who speaks?"

"A friend of mine," Remo told him. "What of it?"

"The one named Youngblood?"

"Yeah. How'd you know that?"

Youngblood snorted like a bull. "Because he's a gook,"
he said. "You've been set up, Remo."

"It is too bad," said Chiun sadly.

"What is?" Remo wanted to know.

"That you have found your long-lost Army friend. It
is very sad."

"Look, Ho. Why don't you take a hike?" Remo suggested. "We've got a lot of catching up to do."

"How can you speak such hard words to one who has
meant so much to you?"

"Easy. I'm dead. Dead people can do whatever they
want."

"Ah, then you remember that you are dead. That is
good."

"It is?"

"Hey, I don't want no part of this conversation,"
Youngblood said hotly. "This is bullshit."

Chiun ignored him. "What else do you remember, Remo?"

"Nothing."

"Nothing?" squeaked Chiun. So Remo did not remember after all. And until he did, Chiun could do nothing with him.

"That's what I said. Now screw off."

"But you do remember that you are dead. You have been dead now for many years."

"Then it's true," Remo said hollowly. "How did you know?"

"Why, because . . ." Chiun began. A thought occurred to the Master of Sinanju. A fable of Remo's upbringing he had once shared with him. "It is because I am your guardian angel. Yes, your illustrious guardian angel. I am here to escort you to where you belong."

"You? My guardian angel is Vietnamese?"

"No, Korean."

"North or South?"

"North, of course."

"My guardian angel is a Communist?"

"No, dense one. Your guardian angel is Sinanju."

"I think there's been some mistake. I'm Catholic."

"Emperor Smith is worried about you."

"Who's Emperor Smith?"

"Why, he is the ruler of America, of course. He sent me to bring you back."

"Did you hear that, Dick? America's turned into a monarchy. Probably because we lost the war, I'll bet. Hey, why would this emperor send someone to bring back a dead man?"

"He's messing with your head, Remo," Youngblood said. "Send him away."

"I am telling the truth," Chiun said haughtily.

"Prove it," Remo snapped.

"How?"

"Get us out of here."

"Why did you not ask before? Wait here."

"For what?"

"I am going to create a distraction to assist your escape."

"Did you hear that, Dick?" Remo said sarcastically. "Uncle Ho is going to create a distraction. If you have anything to pack, now's the time to start."

"I ain't listening to either of you. You're both flipped out."

"Do not worry," promised the Master of Sinanju. "This will not take long. The elephant of surprise is on our side."

After the Master of Sinanju had vanished, Dick Youngblood had a question.

"Did he say 'elephant'?"

"I think he meant 'element.' Like 'element of surprise.' " Remo was looking through the bullet holes eagerly.

"What're you looking at?" Youngblood asked.

"I want to see what he's going to do."

"Do? He's going to go to the camp commander and they're going to drink rice wine and laugh at us until the monsoon season comes. What do you think he's going to do?"

"I don't know," Remo said slowly. "I saw him turn an AK-47 to powder with his bare hands."

Dick Youngblood sat staring at the dimly lit profile of Remo Williams, his bulldog face cocked quizzically.

"You know what I think?" he said at last.

"What?"

"I think I'm asleep and you're my nightmare for tonight. I'm going to catch some shut-eye—even though we both know I'm already asleep. I just hope you and that crazy old gook are gone when I wake up."

The first sound wasn't long in coming. A thatched hut crashed. Remo was unable to see what was happening, but the noise was unmistakable. Bamboo splintered. Dry roof grass crackled as if on fire.

There was yelling, panic, and Vietnamese voices raised in shrill confusion. And in the midst of it all, a bellowing animal sound.

Dick Youngblood jumped to Remo's side.

"What's happening. What's going on?"

"I don't know," Remo said. He moved from vent hole to vent hole, trying to see.

Knifelike fingernails suddenly appeared in a cluster of bullet holes near Remo's face. He recoiled.

"Uncle Ho again!" he cried.

The fingernails slashed down. The sound of steel being sheared hurt their eardrums. Youngblood scurried to the furthest corner of the conex.

"I don't believe what I'm seeing," he said.

One section of the conex wall hung in strips. The strips were swiftly peeled back, opening up a man-size hole.

A wrinkled parchment face poked into the conex interior.

"What are you waiting for?" Chiun inquired. "Come."

Remo didn't hesitate.

"You coming?" he asked Youngblood.

"I know I'm dreaming."

"You can wake up later."

"Or you can die now," Chiun said sharply. "Come."

Youngblood crawled out of the conex, saying, "I read somewhere back in the world that if you die in a dream you're dead when you wake up, so I figure I got nothing to lose."

"This way," said Remo.

The camp was in a panic. Surprisingly, there was no shooting.

"What did you do, Ho?" Remo asked.

"The name is Chiun. I am Master of Sinanju."

"And I'm the King of Siam," Youngblood said.

"You are going to make what I must do easier," Chiun warned.

He led them into the bush. Remo threw himself to the ground. He scrambled back to see through the reeds.

"What's that you said, gook?" Youngblood asked.

"Nothing," Chiun told him. He turned to Remo. "What are you waiting for? We must be gone from this place."

"Lan's still in there."

"My men too," Youngblood added. "I ain't leavin' 'em, either."

"Agreed," said Remo.

"Not agreed," said Chiun. "I rescued you. Therefore you must do as I say."

"I don't remember agreeing to that. You, Dick?"

"Nah, the old gook is crazy anyway. See that barracks hut? Think we can get to it?"

"Maybe. All the commotion seems to be on the other side. Sounds like a tank run amok."

"Tanks don't sound like that thing. You're hearing an animal."

"It is," Chiun said.

"What is?" Remo asked.

Suddenly a spotlight was turned on. It showed a

rearing gray monster. A Vietnamese soldier was scooped up by a snake of flesh and smashed against a wall. A hulking mass descended on a thatched hut. It fell like a house of cards.

"Holy shit!" Youngblood breathed. "That's a fucking elephant."

"Not an elephant," Chiun said with satisfaction. "It is *the* elephant."

"What elephant is that?" Youngblood asked, wide-eyed.

"The elephant of surprise you Americans always speak of."

"What'd I tell you?" Remo said.

"I don't want to hear it. Listen, we gotta get us some weapons. What do you say?"

"I'm game."

"Yes," Chiun said sternly. "You are both dead ducks if you blunder ahead. Wait here, I will find your friends."

"Who put you in charge?" Remo asked, turning around.

There was no reply. Remo nudged Youngblood with an elbow.

"What?"

"Look behind you," Remo suggested.

Youngblood looked. There was no sign of the old Oriental. He groaned.

"Not that spook shit again. I hate this."

"Look," Remo said.

"No way. I ain't looking at nothing. I'm dreaming."

But Dick Youngblood looked anyway. The old Oriental was inside the camp, calmly walking toward the main cluster of buildings. He paused and cupped his hands over his thin lips. A weird cry was emitted.

The elephant trumpeted a reply and lurched away from the camp. It crashed into the bush, its long trunk slapping from side to side. It moved with unbelievable speed.

A pack of Vietnamese soldiers followed it with sticks.

"Why don't they just shoot it?" Remo wondered aloud.

"You kiddin', man? We're in Cambodia. An elephant is like a horse to these slopes. He's a pack animal and a tow truck rolled into one, and if he starts eating too much, you can always shoot him and eat off him for a month."

"They're not going to catch him anytime soon," Remo pointed out. "Let's go."

"I'm with you. *Semper Fi*, do or die."

They charged out of the bush and sought the lee of the long barracks building. The camp was starting to quiet down.

"I'll go first," Youngblood said, peering around the corner.

"If you see a Vietnamese girl with green eyes and freckles, she's friendly," Remo said, pushing him off.

Youngblood's legs churned. For the first time, Remo had a good look at him in bright light. He was heavy. A big man whose muscles had been softened by time and confinement. He looked old. Remo looked at his own smooth hands, wondering how they could belong to someone who was Youngblood's age.

No time to think about that now, Remo thought. He got ready to run.

A safety clicked off directly behind him and Remo felt the flesh over his spine writhe like a snake.

"*Chu hoi!*" the voice of Captain Dai said. It was high-pitched, nervous.

Recognizing an order to surrender, Remo turned slowly, his hands lifting.

"Looks like it's you and me again," Remo said resignedly. Whatever happened, he was going to buy Dick Youngblood enough time to do what he had to.

Captain Dai Chim Sao knew how to make a man talk.

A woman would be easy. He had had the *bui doi* girl, Lan, taken to his office. Her hands were tied behind her back and a bamboo pole inserted under her crooked arms, where it would stretch the shoulder joints in their sockets. That alone was painful enough to make some men talk without further torture.

The girl Lan required more.

Captain Dai used his cigarette. First on the soft palms of her hands. Then on the soles of her feet. He stood behind her, toying with her growing sense of expectation. She couldn't see him apply the smoldering butts. The psychological advantage was enormous.

The girl cried and whimpered. She bit her lips to bloody pulp. She refused to beg. Like the detestable Phong. Once, she swore, and he slapped her face. She spat at him and he slapped her again. Just like Phong. She would pay like Phong too.

It didn't take long to break her. And it was a simple thing that did it. He set her long hair afire with a lighter. She screamed. Dai threw water over her head. What remained of her hair smoldered. Her face, raw now, began to puff up.

"No," she whimpered. "No more. Please."

"My English is poor," Dai told her in Vietnamese. "My question is simple. The American said something about killing me again. What did he mean by that?"

"He told me he killed you during the war with the Americans," Lan sobbed.

"So," said Captain Dai. His eyes were like cold embers.

"I know nothing more," Lan told him through peeling lips.

Dai's eyes refocused.

"You remind me of Phong," he said cruelly.

"I know no Phong."

"I will change that," Dai said, placing his sidearm to her temple. "I will send you to meet him."

He fired a single shot.

Lan fell sideways, her body hanging up on the bamboo pole across her back. Slowly she slipped down it until her head touched the pool of water around her. It began to turn red.

Captain Dai stepped out of the interrogation hut. It was incredible. Somehow, fate had sent to him the one American he'd never dared hope he would face. The man who had murdered his father, the father whose face he now wore with arrogant pride.

Captain Dai strode to the conex. He was oblivious of the sounds of confusion erupting all over the camp. Dimly he recognized the trumpeting of an elephant. An elephant wasn't important on this night. Only the American killer of his father was important.

Captain Dai wrenched down the conex door lever. He threw it open. His set jaw loosened, sending his dangling cigarette to the ground.

The conex was empty. Moonlight filled the interior from a gaping hole.

Frantically Captain Dai raced into the camp. He hoped no one would kill the American before he found him. He prayed to his ancestors that he would not be denied that exquisite pleasure.

When Captain Dai saw the black sergeant blunder out from behind a hut, he slipped around to the other side. His pocked face broke out in ugly joy.

The American was there. He turned slowly.

Captain Dai would have shot him in the back without hesitation. Just as he had done to countless nameless Americans he had ambushed during the war. But he wanted this American to know why he was going to die.

"You killed my father," he told him in Vietnamese.

"My hands *are* up," the American said. "I'm *chu hoing, bien?*"

The idiot did not understand him. It was important that he understand.

"My father NVA, *bien?*" Dai said.

The American shrugged his shoulders.

"You killed him. For that I have killed many Americans. Now I kill you. *Crackadill, bien?*"

The American looked blank. Captain Dai swore. If only he knew the English word for "kill."

The Master of Sinanju freed the prisoners by a simple method. He found the hut where they were imprisoned. It was easy to identify. It was a little way from the others, and had two armed soldiers standing at the entrance.

Chiun slipped up to the back and with a fingernail sliced a low rectangular hatch out of the wall. He slipped in and invited the Americans and Amerasians to accompany him to safety.

"I am sent by the American government," he whispered. "Follow quietly. There is a submarine waiting for us."

They looked at him without comprehension. A ripple of expressions greeted him: doubt, suspicion, fear. They didn't budge.

Chiun nudged them with his lightninglike fingernails.

The pain made the prisoners scramble out of the hut as if it'd been filled with swarming hornets.

Chiun beckoned them to the safety of the bush, and motioned for them to stay hidden. There was still the girl. Naturally, she would be the one who would make the rescue difficult.

Then he saw the black man, Youngblood, lumbering from hut to hut like a bear. Chiun rolled his eyes. Americans. They were like children, never staying where you told them.

He raced after Youngblood and saw Remo standing in the shadow of a building with his hands raised in surrender. A Vietnamese officer had him covered. The Vietnamese was babbling some nonsense at Remo. Chiun could tell by Remo's puzzled expression that he did not understand the Vietnamese's angry words.

"Remo!" Chiun called.

Remo's head turned. He looked frightened.

"Hey, Uncle Ho. Give me a hand here."

Chiun hesitated. He was too far away. If he moved on the Vietnamese, there would be shooting. He did not want to lose Remo to a stupid little rock.

"If you harm my son," Chiun told the officer in his own language, "a terrible death will descend upon you."

"I fear no death, old man."

"I am Sinanju. That white man is also Sinanju. Think hard upon that fact," Chiun intoned.

"Hey, Ho, whatever you're telling him, better stop. He's only getting madder."

"This American killed my father," the Vietnamese told Chiun, and his finger tightened on the trigger.

"I think he's going to shoot, Ho!" Remo yelled.

"Remember your training, Remo," Chiun called sternly.

"What?"

"Your mind calls them bullets, but they are only rocks."

"I'm about to be cut down and you're talking geology."

"You fear the little rock only because your mind tells you to," Chiun went on, stepping forward carefully. "You would not fear a man throwing a big rock at you."

"I fear bullets," Remo said, his eyes fixed on the quivering gun barrel.

"Yes," Chiun said. "That is right. Look at the barrel. Do not take your eyes from it. Relax. Do not move until you see the bullet coming."

"Move? I'm petrified."

"Old man," the Vietnamese said, "tell this American for me that he killed my father, Captain Dai Ma Qui, and I will spare his life."

"Remo," Chiun said, "this idiot says you killed his father."

"Tell him I know," Remo said, his eyes so intent upon the barrel they almost crossed.

"He says he knows," Chiun said.

Captain Dai fired.

"Remember!" Chiun called as he flashed ahead, but Remo did not hear him. The dark gun muzzle filled with fire and smoke, the bullet a grayish blot speeding just a microsecond before them. Remo's head seemed to expand. He was no longer in control of his body. It was moving on its own, moving with a deliberate speed that made the world seem to stand still.

The bullet sped toward Remo's chest. It seemed so slow. Remo jerked aside. The bullet passed him, not an inch from the front of his T-shirt. The sharp bullwhip sound of the bullet's passing was a sharp pain in his ears.

Remo batted the pistol out of the Vietnamese's hands before he could squeeze off a second round. Remo kicked him in the groin, and when he slipped to his knees, clutching himself, Remo knocked his shovellike teeth loose.

Chiun appeared beside him.

"Sloppy. Bad technique."

Remo turned. "Are you kidding? I side-stepped a live round at point-blank range and bashed this clown's face in."

"Why do you not kill him?"

"Can't."

Chiun almost staggered. He braced himself against the building and placed a stricken hand to his breast.

"Can't!" he squeaked. "My son, the assassin who cannot kill. Why not?"

"It's against the Geneva Accords to kill a prisoner."

Chiun blinked. "Against . . ."

Dick Youngblood came up behind them, an AK-47 clutched in his big hands.

"You got him, huh? Guess you'll want me to polish him off for you?"

"What do you mean?" Remo asked.

"I looked for your girlfriend, Remo. I found her."

Remo's face went stony. His mouth parted. Nothing came out.

"She was in his personal interrogation room. Looks like he tortured her before he shot her. I'm sorry, man."

Remo's lips formed the name Lan. The sound wasn't even a breath. Woodenly he turned to face Captain Dai. Still clutching himself, Dai looked up at Remo with a face that possessed all the agony of twisting, hot metal. His rage radiated like spilt slag.

Remo reached down and took Captain Dai by his collar. He lifted him off his feet effortlessly. Captain Dai hung with his boots not touching the ground. Remo cocked a fist. His fist hovered before Dai's face, quivering as if all of Remo's energy was being focused into it.

When Remo let fly, there came a crack like a baseball bat connecting for a home run, and suddenly Captain Dai's head was no longer there. His sheared stalk of a neck pumped like a scarlet fountain.

Remo dropped the corpse. There was no sign anywhere of the head. Then, out of the bush, came a series of noises like a coconut falling through heavy foliage. It ended with a soft *thunk*. Then there was silence.

Dick Youngblood disappeared around a corner and got audibly sick.

Chiun examined Remo's fist. There wasn't a mark on it. Not even a drop of blood.

"Better," he said firmly. "I thought you couldn't kill him."

"I remembered something."

"Yes?"

"The North Vietnamese never signed the Geneva Accords."

"Is that all?"

"What else should I remember?"

"We will find that out later," said Chiun abruptly. "Come. We must leave this place."

Chiun led them to the bush where the American POW's and the Amerasians were hiding. Youngblood cut off their questions and got them organized.

"Listen up. The old guy's gonna lead us out of here. Don't give him no shit. Got that?"

"We cannot walk," Chiun told them. "We must have a vehicle."

"I'll grab a tank," Remo said. Without another word, he disappeared.

The tank came lumbering up moments later. Remo's head stuck up from the driver's hatch.

When Dick Youngblood saw it, he started swearing.

"Williams, you idiot!" he yelled. "That's the T-54. The cannon ain't real."

"Someone ran off with the other one," Remo told him.

"Well, it's better than nothing," Youngblood grumbled. "Let's hope we don't have to do no fighting."

Those who couldn't fit inside the tank clung to the deck. Chiun took a commanding position in the turret hatch.

He pointed south and called, "Forward!" Then he folded his arms imperiously.

Remo looked up at him sourly. "Who died and left you in charge, Chiun?"

"I am merely pointing the way to the waiting submarine," Chiun said defensively. Then, reacting, he added, "Chiun! You called me Chiun!"

"Of course," Remo said blandly. "That's your name, isn't it?"

Chiun eyed the back of Remo's head wonderingly.

Along the way, they came upon the elephant. The elephant was calmly tramping a circle in the middle of the jungle path. The circle was greenish and soaked in red, like a blanket that had been drenched in cranberry juice. Except that from the edges of the mushy patch human hands and limbs protruded. They did not move. They were attached to a communal blob.

Chiun whispered and the elephant fell in behind the tank.

"Do not worry," Chiun said when the prisoners started to scramble for the front of the tank in fear. "He is on our side. I told him I would lead him to a nice place if he helped us."

"You can talk to elephants?" Remo asked.

"Mostly I listen. This is a very friendly elephant. I found him dragging a cannon. Peasant fighters were flogging him. I needed transportation because you denied me a ride in your tank, and dragging a cannon is a waste of a good elephant. So I liberated him."

"What's his name?"

"I call him Rambo."

"Don't you mean Dumbo?"

Chiun eyed Remo warily. "Are you certain your memory has not returned?"

"Why would it do a strange thing like that?" Remo asked innocently.

21

The defense minister of the Socialist Republic of Vietnam put down the phone and walked back to the tactical table on which a plastic map of Southeast Asia lay flat.

Grimly he moved a black counter closer to the open sea. In a ragged line behind the counter, many red counters were strewn.

"They have a destination in mind," he told his top general, the only other man in the Hanoi operations room. "It is either a village or port. If they sought mere escape, they would have fled deeper into Cambodia, not back into Vietnam."

"A village or seaport on the Gulf of Thailand, obviously," General Trang said. "I will have the entire coast sealed off."

The defense minister shook his iron-gray head.

"No, we will let them reach the gulf. It may be that there are American rescue ships waiting off the coast."

"We could stop them before that, and wring the truth from their weak lips."

"These red counters," the defense minister said bitterly, "represent the latest Soviet military equipment. Modern tanks, Hind gunships, and self-propelled howitzers. This black counter is an old T-54 with a cannon that cannot even fire. Why do we move the black counter every hour, but every red counter we move into position stops dead?"

The general blinked. He wondered if the question was a rhetorical one. He decided to answer anyway.

"Because they have been destroyed, Comrade Defense Minister."

"Because they have been destroyed," the defense minister said woodenly. "Exactly. Everything we throw at them bogs down or falls from the sky. How is it possible?"

"I do not know."

"One tank. One American tourist. A handful of undernourished U.S. prisoners of war and an unknown number of mongrel *bui doi* armed with assault rifles and limited ammunition. Yet they win."

General Trang cleared his throat. "I am told they also have an elephant," he ventured lamely.

The defense minister raised a skeptical eyebrow. He shook his head silently. "This reminds me of the war."

"Which war?" the general asked reasonably.

"The war against the Americans."

"But we won that war."

"That is what worries me. We were the thorn in the side of a huge military machine. We expected to lose. And because we knew we would fail anyway, we kept fighting, for we had only the choice of victory or death."

"I do not follow, comrade."

"We beat the Americans for one fundamental reason. We cared more about winning than they did. But these," he said, tapping the black counter, "are not fighting for the glory of victory. They are fighting for their lives."

"But this time we are the huge military machine," General Trang protested.

"Yes. Exactly. That is what worries me. Summon a gunship to take me to the area. I will personally manage the ground campaign," he ordered. "If it is not too late," he added.

"But . . . but this is just a skirmish."

"So were Waterloo, Dien Bien Phu, and Khe Sanh,"

said the defense minister, picking up the ringing telephone with a distasteful expression, knowing that it would be more bad news. "The Tet offensive was a hundred skirmishes happening at once. None were decisive. In fact we lost most of those skirmishes. Yet it turned the tide against the Americans. I just hope we are not on the wrong side of this particular skirmish." He felt suddenly very old.

Remo sent the tank into the bush. Its tracks chewed up elephant grass until it reached a tree line. He braked and pulled himself out of the driver's cockpit.

"Gather up as much foliage as you can to cover the tank," he ordered.

"You heard the man," Dick Youngblood barked as he wriggled out of the turret. "Let's move, move, move. We ain't home yet."

The Amerasians got busy. Of the former prisoners of war, all but the ailing Colletta pitched in.

"You really kept up the discipline," Remo said admiringly as they broke branches and made a pile for the others to carry to the tank.

Youngblood cracked a wide grin. "You know it. When the last real officer died, morale was bad. That was when I turned into a real hardass. If I caught a man talking Vietnamese, I'd whip his raggedy ass. For a while it was rough on the men. I was pushing 'em one way and the gooks another."

"What happened?"

"Everybody found out I was meaner. The gooks started leanin' on me instead of the men, but I could take it. They'd starve me, but I was such a mother I wouldn't lose weight, just to spite them. They'd stick me in that ol' conex and when they'd come to get me out, I'd smile into their ugly faces and say thanks for the ride."

Remo grinned. "Same old Youngblood."

"Feel like Oldblood now, Remo. I've been holding

out so long that now I can see freedom in sight, I just don't know if I have the strength to make it through the homestretch."

"Listen. We'll make it. Chiun will see to that."

"You got a whole new attitude toward ol' Uncle Ho now that we're on the loose."

"He should be catching up with us any minute," Remo said, looking around. "Listen, do me a favor. Stop calling me Remo."

"Why? It's your name, ain't it? Or did you forget that too?"

"I can't explain. And don't use the name in front of the men, either. You and Chiun are the only ones who know who I am. Let's keep it that way."

"Now, what the hell difference does that make?"

"A life-or-death difference. Just trust me."

"Okay, you're the man. Hey, don't this remind you of the time you stole that gook tank and ran it all the way to . . . Now, what was the name of that little shithole hamlet?"

"Phuc Hu."

"Yeah. That's what we called it, all right. You know, rememberin' you drive that sucker in that day, with our side itching to blow you away thinkin' you was Charlie— that was one memory that kept me going all these years. Funny what a man clings to when he's down to zero."

"I remember Khe Sanh a lot better."

"Yeah, Khe Sanh. It all changed after that, didn't it? And Tet. You remember Tet?"

"Yeah," Remo said, searching the road with troubled eyes. "I remember Tet."

They finished camouflaging the tank. The men began settling down. Remo set two Amerasians on sentry duty because they were fresher.

"Shit," Youngblood said, sitting down and putting his back against the grass-entangled treads. "Tet. Hey, you remember that cocksucker of a major we had at Khe Sanh? What's-his-name?"

"You mean Bauer?"

"Yeah. That was his name. Deke Bauer. Everyone hated him. Meanest sonovabitch I ever met. I used to lie awake in that conex and wonder whatever happened to him. Sometimes I'd make up grisly ways for him to buy it, just to pass the time."

"He died," Remo said distantly.

"Our side or theirs?"

"Neither. He bought it back in the world."

"The world. Man, I last saw the world when I was twenty. I'm over forty now. Nam sure took a big chunk of this old Leatherneck's life. Wonder if I can hack it back there now."

Youngblood suddenly looked up at Remo with skeptical eyes. "How'd you know Bauer bought it back in the world? I thought you couldn't remember nothing but Nam."

Remo didn't answer for the longest time. Then he spoke. "Here comes Chiun. Remember what I said about using my name."

But Dick Youngblood didn't reply. His eyes were closed and his big bulldog face had settled into sleep.

Remo went to greet the Master of Sinanju. Chiun came riding in on the back of his elephant. Chiun tapped the elephant's flank with a short length of bamboo and the elephant stopped and knelt. Chiun dismounted.

"You did not need to wait," Chiun told him. "Rambo and I would have caught up to you."

"We need rest," Remo said simply.

"We need to reach the American submarine," said Chiun. "If it is discovered by the Vietnamese, it may leave without us, and then where would we be?"

"In Vietnam," Remo said simply. "Where a lot of us

have been for a long, long time. Anything else would be a step up. Even dead."

"You seem more at ease than I have seen you in a while," Chiun pointed out.

Remo looked away. "Why not? We're almost to the coast."

"I mean with me."

"You got us out. I'm not worried about you anymore."

"But your face is not entirely free from worry."

"Don't you think it's time to get rid of the elephant? He's slowing us down."

"I promised him a nice home when this is over."

"He won't fit in the submarine."

"That remains to be seen," Chiun said.

"Have it your way, Little—" Remo abruptly walked away.

Chiun bounced after him. "What did you say?"

"I said have it your way, you little gook," Remo said hotly. "I just don't want my people jeopardized because you insist on having your way about everything. Got that?"

Chiun stopped in his tracks. "Yes," he said softly. "I have it. I have it perfectly."

Hours later, a Hind gunship orbited by. It flew higher than the last few, which had all gone down in flames under the concentrated fire of their AK-47's. The tanks had long ago stopped turning up in the road. Not all the machine-gun fire in the world could affect them, but each tank that had gotten in their way had been confronted by the Master of Sinanju. Treads had been popped, cannon bores bent double, and hatches smashed shut. They rolled past each piece of wreckage with impunity.

"Looks like he ain't sticking around," Youngblood told Remo.

Remo watched the gunship disappear beyond some

hills. "He couldn't have missed spotting the elephant," he replied. "We'd better get on the move again."

They pushed south along the completely deserted road. Not even the occasional conical-hatted farmer could be seen.

Dick Youngblood shoved his head into the driver's pit.

"They know we're on this road," he whispered. "No doubt about it."

"What do you think?"

"There's two ways this could go. One, they've given up and are lettin' us go. The other is that they're massing somewhere ahead for an ambush."

"The Vietnamese don't know about giving up."

"Well, there you go," Youngblood said quietly. "Been real nice knowing you, Remo."

"I've come a long way for you," Remo said. "I'm getting you home."

"Well, I've been talkin' to your gook friend and he's sayin' there may not be room on the sub for all of us. He keeps lookin' at me when he says that. Why's he doing that?"

"He's not a gook, and don't worry about Chiun. I can handle him."

"Yeah, while you're handling him, who's going to be handling whatever the Vietnamese are getting ready to throw at us?"

Remo grinned. "I thought I'd leave that little detail to you."

Youngblood slapped Remo on the back boisterously. "Always said you were a generous man. Glad to see that much ain't changed."

They rolled on through the night, pausing only to allow Chiun and his elephant to catch up. The sound of the tank's noisy motor beat down on Remo's concentration. He ran with the hatches open because the oil stink was getting to his sensitive nostrils.

Every few hours a helicopter gunship prowled above. But they were unmolested. It was very ominous.

The tangy scent of seawater crept into the air just as dawn was breaking. Remo began to worry. They were nearing their destination, if Chiun's directions were on the mark, but there had been no sign of the Master of Sinanju in many hours.

Remo sent the tank around a long bend in the road that ran through the middle of a rubber-tree plantation. A figure stepped out onto the road and cocked a thumb like a hitchhiker.

"Chiun!"

"Who else?" asked the Master of Sinanju, leaping onto the moving tank. The Amerasians squatting on the superstructure moved aside to make room for him.

"Where's the elephant?" Remo wondered.

"We took a shortcut and I saw danger so I sent him ahead."

"Bait, eh?"

"Remo! Your memory may not know me, but I would think your judgment would tell you that this sweet face would never harm a worthy animal."

"Okay," Remo said. "What are we getting into?"

"Many soldiers, many tanks. And the helicopter things."

"How many?"

"Many, many."

"That's a lot."

"They are on the beach we seek. I do not know about the submarine. I could not see it."

"Let me know when we're getting close," Remo said grimly.

"You have a plan, perhaps?"

"I have an objective. I'm going to reach it, plan or no plan."

The Master of Sinanju sniffed disdainfully.

"Rambo talk again. It will take years to purge you of it, and I am already an old man. Fie!"

"No," Remo said. *"Semper Fi."*

Dick Youngblood's voice sang out from the tank's innards. "Do or die!"

22

The defense minister ordered the Hind gunship pilot to make a final pass over the slow-moving T-54 tank. It looked like such an ineffectual object, with tiny figures clinging to its superstructure.

Obviously, he thought, it was not the machine, but the men inside. He ordered the pilot to return to the staging area.

It would have been a beautiful stretch of white beach but it swarmed with soldiers in fatigues and a ranked mass of T-72 tanks and a few of the older T-64's. They were lined up at the shore, tread-to-tread, their smooth-bore cannon all pointing in the same direction. Inland. Toward the shore end of the road.

In one way, the assembled might of the Vietnamese Army was beautiful in the defense minister's eyes as he stepped from the settling gunship and marched under the watchful eyes of the tank commanders, his holstered sidearm slapping his thigh.

General Trang snapped a salute in greeting.

"They are less than a kilometer away," the defense minister told him.

"They have no chance, as you can see."

"They have cut a scar down half the countryside already. Do not underestimate them—especially when they are close to their objective."

"And what objective is that? I see no rescue craft."

"Our patrol boats report sonar soundings in the bay. Very large sonar soundings."

General Trang's face grew grim. "A submarine?"

"I have ordered depth charges dropped on it," said the defense minister, climbing atop a tank for a better view of the harbor.

"Dare we risk it?"

The defense minister looked down at him coldly. "We have won the military war with the Americans," he said. "But we have lost the economic war. Our industrial base is a shambles. Our money is worthless. We have no potable water anymore. We have enemies on all borders and our supposed friends the Russians, who are like the Americans except they have no money to spend, are leeching us dry. One day soon, we may have to fight them too."

"None of what you say is new to me, comrade."

"But obviously you have not applied your brain to the political situation. Let me do that for you. Our only hope lies with our former enemies, the Americans. Only their friendship and economic assistance can save Vietnam. We must have their goodwill, even if we have to achieve it by force."

"I understand. We can never get it if the American prisoners escape on their own."

"It is too late even to return them under a pretext," the defense minister said. "Thanks to that bungler Captain Dai. The Americans must all perish. Here, on this beach. By sundown."

The defense minister abruptly stopped speaking. Rumbling detonations came from out in the bay.

"But the American submarine, which has violated our territorial waters, may be the card that achieves our objective," he said. More detonations followed. Then, like a whale coming up for air, the submarine surfaced. Its conning tower broke the surface of the bay, throwing up spray. It settled.

"We have them!" General Trang said excitedly when the American-flag emblem on the conning tower became visible.

"And we will offer them back to America—in return for certain voluntary economic concessions," said the defense minister. "Once the POW problem is totally resolved."

"I can send my tanks forward, crushing everything in their path," General Trang suggested eagerly.

"No," said the defense minister, dropping to the sand. "Let the tank come. When they see we have their submarine, they will know they have no hope of escaping our shores. We will offer surrender terms. They will accept. And we will eliminate them."

"Stop here," ordered the Master of Sinanju.

Remo braked the tank. "Everyone sit tight," he called out. "I'm going to see what we're up against."

Remo shinned up a banana tree. From his perch he saw it all, the tanks, the grounded gunships waiting to lift off, and out in the blue waters of the Gulf of Thailand, a U.S. submarine—dead in the water and surrounded by the red-flagged patrol boats.

When his feet touched the ground, Remo's face was ashen. Everybody saw it.

"They've captured the sub," Remo said simply.

The prisoners groaned in a single voice. Some wept. A few threw down their weapons in frustration. Youngblood stamped his feet like an overgrown child.

"Damn!" he said bitterly.

"You no longer have an objective, never mind a plan," Chiun told Remo coolly. "What will you do now, soldier boy?"

"Win," said Remo.

"How?" asked Youngblood. The others echoed him.

Remo turned to Chiun. "I'll bet you can handle those patrol boats."

The Master of Sinanju looked at Remo pointedly. "And what makes you think a frail old man such as myself could manage that daunting task?"

"I've seen you in action before. Can you?"

Chiun bowed. "Of course—for a modest price."

Remo's face clouded.

"What?" he said tightly.

"It is no great thing. I only wish your help in transporting my elephant to America."

Relief washed over Remo's face. "You got it," he said.

Remo faced the others. "While he's doing that, we have to get past the beach. They have tanks and helicopters, but we've beaten them before. Are you with me?"

"Hell, yes!" they shouted.

"Then let's do it!" Remo said. "Anytime you're ready, Chiun."

But Chiun was already gone.

The Master of Sinanju took the direct approach. With scores of tank cannon and rifle muzzles converging at the end of the road, he did the unexpected. He simply walked out of the jungle.

The Vietnamese were expecting Americans. They expected a powerless tank. They did not expect a venerable Asian man in a ridiculous kimono striding calmly toward their lines. His hands were empty, so they did not fire.

The defense minister stepped up to the old Asian.

Insultingly, the old Asian walked right past him. At the defense minister's order, soldiers reached out to arrest him. They fell on their faces, their hands clutching beach sand.

The old Asian walked past the tanks and into the surf. He continued walking until his head disappeared under the waves.

While all eyes watched the venerable old man vanish so mysteriously, gunfire erupted from inland.

The defense minister dived for cover. He ordered the general to return fire. The general ordered return fire from behind a tank.

The smooth-bore cannon started shelling. The noise was deafening. Trees crashed. Dust geysered upward. The defense minister shouted for the gunships to take off, but he couldn't be heard. The gunships began collecting bullet holes from the sporadic fire of the unseen Americans.

Finally one did lift off of its own accord, the pilot frightened into action. The helicopter started to swarm away from the beach and out to sea, but it never reached the water. A storm of rounds stitched its cockpit and riddled the weapons pod. An antitank rocket ignited. The helicopter turned into a shower of flame and hot, slicing metal.

Several tanks directly beneath the plummeting gunship were smothered in flaming fuel. Soldiers fled the tanks. The burning fuel raced along the sand. Desperately the other tanks surged ahead, trying to get clear. They smashed into one another, treads gnashing treads. One tank, running blind, actually climbed the superstructure of another and tipped over like an upended turtle. It fell on the screaming body of General Trang.

It was out of control. And all because of that old man who had seemingly committed suicide. The defense minister hunkered down behind the tank line, trying to figure out a way to make his men cease fire. Burning smoke seared his lungs. His eyes smarted. He plunged into the surf for relief, thinking that it was like Dien Bien Phu all over again. But in reverse.

Remo gave the cease-fire order.

"Tell them to conserve ammo," he told Youngblood. The word was passed down the line.

"Casualties our side?" Remo whispered.

The word came back through Youngblood. "None."

"Casualties their side?"

"Heavy," Youngblood told him amiably. "And gettin'
heavier. Sounds like they're doing each other."

"Okay," Remo said. "I'm going to see how Chiun is
doing."

Remo went up a tree. The top had been sheared off
by a shellburst. Most of the shells had landed further
inland, where the T-54 had been left. The Vietnamese
had set their range on it, as Remo had assumed. Mirac-
ulously, it had survived. He'd brought his men up close
to the tree line—much closer than the Vietnamese would
have expected. It had worked. They avoided the cannon shells, their biggest worry.

Out in the gulf, Remo saw three patrol boats circling
the wallowing submarine. He grinned tightly. Before,
there had been four boats. As he watched, one slipped
under the water, stern-first. It went down as if pulled
by unseen fingers. Remo spied the colorful figure of
Chiun swimming from the vortex of the sinking boat to
the next-nearest craft.

As Remo watched, the Master of Sinanju pressed up
against the stern of that boat. He could be seen jabbing
his fingers into the hull below the waterline. Remo
could almost imagine the punch-press sound of his fingers piercing the hull.

The third patrol boat disappeared with all hands.

Remo dropped to the ground.

"Okay, the sub will be in the clear by the time we hit
the beach."

"How are we gonna do that?" an American demanded.
"We're still outnumbered."

"The same way Chiun did. March right down to the
water and swim for it."

"But they'll zap us for sure."

"Our tank made it. I'll use it to create a diversion.

They'll open up on me. While I keep them busy, every-one slips into the water at the far end. They're so confused down there, it should be a piece of cake."

"Good plan," Youngblood said. "Except for one thing."

Remo looked at him.

"I'm drivin' the tank."

"Nothing doing," Remo said. "It's too dangerous."

"I sure ain't walkin' down. I'm too old. Can't outrun the bullets like I usta."

"I'm with the sarge," Boyette piped up. "After all he's done for us, he deserves a free ride."

"Shit, I ain't lookin' for no free ride," Youngblood protested. "I just know I'm the man for the job, is all." He looked at Remo intently. "Unless someone thinks he knows a better man than me."

"Not me," said Remo, shaking his head.

"They're gonna need you to save their raggedy butts," Youngblood whispered to Remo. "I carried 'em this far. I'm countin' on you gettin' them home."

"We're all goin' home," Remo shot back.

"I hear you," said Youngblood. And without another word he charged back to the tank. Its rumbling engine started up immediately.

The old T-54 rolled past them and Dick Youngblood shot them a lazy wave of the hand before he buttoned up the driver's hatch and sent the grinding machine sliding down to the beach.

"There goes a man," a voice said.

"Amen."

"Save the prayers for church," Remo barked, his eyes anxious. "Dick won't be able to buy us much time. We go in twos. Starting—"

The gunfire started up again. The sounds of bullets ricocheting wildly off plate metal came to their ears.

"Now!" Remo said, pushing the first two off.

He watched as they worked down the tree line,

running parallel with the T-54. They reached the water unseen and unhurt.

"Next!" Remo yelled.

And so it went. The first three teams got to the water while the Vietnamese peppered the T-54 with machine-gun fire. By then Youngblood's tank was cannon-to-cannon with a heavier T-72.

"What does he do?" someone asked. Remo noticed it was one of the Amerasians, Nguyen.

It became immediately apparent what Youngblood was up to. When the T-54 cannon barrel rammed the heavier smoothbore, the dummy bore began to splinter. The tanks kept lurching at each other.

But out of the driver's hatch, Dick Youngblood arose like a genie from a lamp. He leapt to the other tank and popped its turret hatch, raking the interior with his AK-47.

Then he disappeared inside.

"That hulking sonovabitch," Boyette said in awe.

Youngblood, obviously in command of the T-72, sent the cannon swiveling toward the remaining line of tanks. He began firing. Shells coughed out explosively. The concussions hurt their ears.

"Now!" Remo yelled, jumping to his feet. "Everybody!"

They raced for the beach. There was so much noise and smoke and confusion that even if they were seen, they were a minor factor compared with the rampaging T-72. Remo made sure everyone got into the water before he turned to see about Youngblood.

Youngblood's tank was indistinguishable from the others. It was like bumper cars played with military equipment. Tanks rammed one another blindly. Men ran in all directions. The Vietnamese military had reverted to its fundamental mind-set: every man for himself.

Remo was about to plunge in when one of the American POW's began calling for help. Remo turned. It was Colletta. Too weak to swim, he was going under.

Remo hesitated momentarily, but in the end he had no choice. He plunged in after Colletta.

Gripping the man's chin in the accepted rescue headlock, Remo swam for the sub. All around him, the others were paddling for their lives, their weapons left behind.

Chiun's head bobbed up to one side.

"Take this guy, will you?" Remo asked him.

Seawater squirted from Chiun's mouth. "Why?"

"I've got to go back. Youngblood's still on the beach."

Chiun looked to shore. Each time a shell or tank exploded, a ball of fire climbed heavenward like a raging fist and a wave of heat struck their faces.

"If your friend is there, he is lost."

"Take him!" Remo spat.

Reluctantly the Master of Sinanju took charge of the semiconscious Colletta. Remo struck back for shore.

By the time he stepped onto the open sand, the conflict had settled down. Broken, flaming tanks lay strewn everywhere. The one surviving gunship sat like a broken dragonfly, abandoned and shot to pieces. It had never gotten off the ground.

Remo ran from tank to tank, avoiding gasoline fires, and kicked hatches open in a vain effort to find his friend.

"Dick!" he called. "Dick! Damn!"

Remo found Dick Youngblood half in and half out of the driver's hatch of one T-72, his face pressed to the deck.

Remo turned him over. His face was gray and bloodless, his eyes open as if seeing everything and nothing at the same time.

Frantically Remo pulled Youngblood onto the deck. He slammed his doubled fists over the man's heart. "Come on, come on," he said, applying mouth-to-mouth. Dick's breath smelled like a pulled tooth.

Youngblood suddenly coughed. His eyes fluttered. His lips moved weakly.

"Give it up, man," he whispered. "I'm gone."

"No!" Remo shouted. "I came all this way for you. Breathe!"

"Hey, give it a rest." Youngblood's voice was gentle.

"Phong died for you, dammit," Remo said, shaking him. "Don't you understand? I left you behind the first time. I won't do it again. This can't all have been for nothing."

"It ain't, man. It ain't, 'cause I'm dying free." Then the breath went out of Youngblood's body in a slow, deflating rush.

"Dick . . ." Remo said, hugging the man tightly. "You waited so long. So damn long. Why did it have to be you? Why couldn't it have been one of the others?"

When the tears stopped, Remo pulled the body of his friend free. Dick Youngblood's massive body, for all its bulk, felt strangely light in his arms—as if the best part of him had deserted the physical shell.

With unseeing eyes, Remo walked toward the surf. He was oblivious of the sight of his fellow Americans climbing into the submarine's deck hatches. He didn't notice the man with the iron-gray hair and military bearing crawl out from under a disabled tank, pick up a fallen Kalashnikov rifle from the sand, and point it at his back.

"You!" the man called in heavily accented English.

"Go away," Remo said dully. "It's over."

"I order you to surrender."

"Who are you to order me to do anything?" Remo asked stonily.

"I am the defense minister of the Socialist Republic of Vietnam."

Remo stopped suddenly. An odd light leapt into his eyes.

"That means you're in charge of the Vietnamese military, doesn't it?"

"Yes. Now, drop that man. Quickly!"

Remo did as he was told. He placed Dick Young-blood's body on the sand with infinite care. He turned to face the man with the iron-gray hair.

"You speak English?" Remo asked.

"I participated in the Paris peace talks."

"Then you're just the man I want to talk to," Remo said, advancing grimly.

"I cannot allow you to live," cried the defense minister. And he opened up. Remo veered to one side, evading the bullet stream. The second burst was corrected for his new position, but he wasn't there either. The Kalashnikov ejected its last smoking cartridge. Remo let the fact that the weapon was empty sink into the man's astonished mind.

Then Remo took the rifle and reduced it to splinters and metal grit.

Remo jammed the defense minister of the Socialist Republic of Vietnam up against a decapitated tank. He rifled his pockets, finding a wallet. The wallet contained several folded sheets of paper.

"These will do," Remo said.

"What do you mean?" the defense minister sputtered.

"Can you write English as well as you speak it?"

"Perhaps."

Remo scrounged through the man's pockets until he found a pen. He turned the man around and slapped the paper and pen onto the tank's flat superstructure.

"Write," Remo ordered.

"What shall I write?"

"A surrender treaty. Unconditional surrender."

"I do not understand."

"You were part of the Paris talks. You signed a treaty there. This treaty will replace that one. The terms are simple. Unconditional surrender to the American forces. Me."

"Such a coerced document can mean nothing."

"Humor me," Remo said, forcing his finger into the small of the man's back, where it caused the lower vertebrae to grind together painfully. The defense minister gasped for breath. He began writing.

When he was done, he handed the scraps of paper to Remo with shaky hands. His eyes were stricken.

"It means nothing," he repeated.

"Wrong," Remo told him. "The first treaty meant nothing, because your people never intended to live up to it. But this one is different. It means my friend lying over there died for something. I don't call that nothing."

"Am I your prisoner?"

"I don't take prisoners," Remo told him. Then he released the man's vertebrae. The defense minister fell to the sand with his lungs expelling a final gusty breath.

Remo walked away from the body without a second glance and stood over the mortal remains of Dick Youngblood.

He looked at the papers in his hands and realized that he would have to make a choice. Dick's body or the papers. He couldn't swim with Dick's body in tow and still hold the treaty papers above the ruinous salt water.

Remo was about to drop the papers when the Master of Sinanju called out to him. Remo looked.

Chiun was returning to shore on the back of the elephant he called Rambo.

"The submarine is leaving now," Chiun told him emotionlessly. "Do you wish to come along?"

"Is there room for Dick on that thing's back?"

"He is dead."

"So?"

"So I do not understand. We can do nothing more for him. Why bring his remains back?"

"You'll never understand," Remo said levelly, hoisting Youngblood's body onto the elephant's back. "I'm a Marine, and we don't leave our dead behind."

23

The morning sun sent splinters of light through the skylight of the Folcroft gymnasium as the Master of Sinanju finished screwing the drum magazine into the old Thompson submachine gun.

When the expected knock came at the door, Chiun squeaked pleasantly, "Who is it?"

"It's me. Remo."

"Come in, Remo," Chiun called, and when the door opened, he set himself. The machine gun stuttered like a typewriter hooked up to a quadraphonic sound system.

Remo saw the bullets spewing toward him and weaved out of the way. A line of splinters chewed up the pine floor at his heels.

"Chiun! What are you doing?" Remo called. The bullet track chased him hungrily.

Remo hit the wall moving. He zipped into a running vertical just as the wall started spitting out chunks of bullet-chipped brick. Remo got all the way across the ceiling, running upside down, when the drum ran empty.

He slammed into the wall, scrambled in midair, and started to fall. Somehow, his scuffling feet found traction. He ran down the wall and landed lightly on his feet.

His face was a mask of fury.

"What were you trying to do, kill me?" he accused.

"You ascend the dragon well for a man who has forgotten Sinanju," Chiun replied blandly.

"Oh," said Remo, looking back at the riddled ceiling.

Dr. Harold W. Smith poked his ash-white face into the room.

"Is it safe now?" he asked of no one in particular.

"Come in, Smitty. I was just about to break the news to Chiun."

"What news?" Chiun demanded.

"Remo has his memory back," Smith told him.

"I have just proven that," Chiun said, dropping the tommy gun.

"It came back this morning," Remo said. He snapped his fingers. "Just like that." His face was open and guileless.

Chiun scowled at him. "So easily."

"Smith said it would probably be a temporary thing."

Chiun stepped up to Remo and regarded his blank face inquisitively. "Are you certain you remember everything?"

"Everything," Remo affirmed.

"Good," said Chiun, taking him by the elbow. Remo howled in anguish, clutching his funny bone. As he bent double, Chiun grasped him by an earlobe. His long nails clenched. Remo screamed louder.

"This is for leaving without telling me," Chiun recited.

"Owww!"

"This is for shattering my inviolate word in front of my emperor."

Remo fell to his knees. "Yeowww. Please, Little Father."

"And this is for calling me a gook."

"I didn't mean—"

"And as punishment, it will be your permanent responsibility to hose down my faithful elephant twice daily. But first you atone for your misdeeds by spending a week on Fortress Folcroft's roof, without food, your chest bare to the cruel elements—which are less cruel than you."

"Master of Sinanju," Smith said frantically, "I really don't think you should blame Remo for any of that."

"Not blame Remo!" Chiun squeaked. "And whom should I blame, if not Remo? Are you one of those Americans who insist it is the parents' fault when a child goes astray?"

"Not really," Smith said. "It's just that we cannot hold Remo responsible for his actions. He was having a flashback."

"Yes," Chiun said imperiously, letting Remo go. Remo rubbed his sore earlobe. "His backflash. The question is: did he backflash before he left these shores—or after?"

"I don't remember," Remo said quickly.

"I believe him," Smith said.

"Pauughh!" Chiun spat. "And I suppose you believe this convenient story that he simply woke up this morning with his memory back?"

"It's plausible."

"Besides," Remo said, "I did everyone a favor. The Vietnamese were trying to stick it to us. I stuck them back."

"I've been on the phone with the President," Smith said. "The POW's and the Amerasians have all been debriefed. Their story is that they were rescued by an elderly Vietnamese who led them to the American submarine. They don't know Remo, except by sight. And the POW's think he's another missing-in-action serviceman who happened to be transferred to the prisoner camp prior to the escape. The Amerasians know differently, of course, but they have agreed to leave Remo's early role out of this, and just as a precaution, never to appear on the The Copra Inisfree Show. It was fortunate that Remo entered Vietnam under another name. That's how it will go down in the history books."

Chiun spoke up. "A minor boon, Emperor. When

they write those records, may I be properly known as a Korean, not a Vietnamese?"

"I'm sorry. That would destroy our cover story."

"Then be certain they leave my name out of it entirely," Chiun said bitterly. And he left the room in a huff.

"What about the treaty?" Remo asked after Chiun had gone.

"I spoke with the President about that too. Worthless, I'm afraid," he said, digging the papers from his suit pocket. Remo took them.

"Even when we win, they don't let us win, do they?" he said.

Smith cleared his throat. "I thought you'd want to know that Youngblood has been interred in Arlington National Cemetery with full military honors."

"He deserved better. He deserved to live."

"Try to put it out of your mind."

"I wish you had told me about the service. I would have gone."

"And I would not have let you," Smith said, pausing at the door.

"I feel like I should do something more."

"Security comes first."

The door closed on Remo's muttered curse.

At the Vietnam Veterans' Memorial in Washington, D.C., the custodian was clearing the grounds of the day's litter. There was surprisingly little, considering how many people passed before the twin black-granite walls each day. It made the custodian's job that much easier, but more important, it made him feel good that Americans once again respected their war dead.

As he made a last sweep of the area, he noticed a man crouched before one of the two 250-foot-long angled slabs on which the names of the over fifty-eight thousand U.S. servicemen killed in Vietnam were carved.

The man's fingers touched the highly reflective surface the way he had seen many do when they came to a familiar name.

Quietly the custodian withdrew. The man was probably looking at the name of an old war buddy or relative and deserved to be left in peace.

A little while later, the custodian noticed the man leaving. Despite the bitterness of the Washington winter, he didn't seem cold in his black T-shirt. The custodian nodded in greeting as he passed, and the man nodded back. He had the deadest eyes the custodian had ever seen. Those eyes made him shiver in a way the stark memorial never had. The guy was probably a vet himself. He had that look. What did they call it? Oh, yeah. The thousand-yard stare.

Finishing his work, the custodian paused at the section of the wall where the dead-eyed man had crouched. Impulsively he crouched in the same place. He was surprised to find himself staring at the blank section of the wall reserved for the name of missing servicemen whose fates had yet to be determined.

At the bottom of the row of names, there was a new name. It didn't look like the others. It was not neatly carved and the lettering wasn't of professional quality. A fresh pile of granite dust lay on the ground under the name. Loose grains sifted down from the irregular letters.

The custodian read the name:

RICHARD YOUNGBLOOD, USMC
SEMPER FI

The custodian decided that if anyone asked, he had no idea when or how that unauthorized name got there. He just knew it belonged there as much as any of the others. Maybe more so.

What he could never figure out was how the dead-eyed man had carved the name. He hadn't carried any tools.